Ju
F
H73   Holman, Felice.
b   The murderer.

The Murderer

The Murderer
by Felice Holman

CHARLES SCRIBNER'S SONS, NEW YORK

Copyright © 1978 Felice Holman

Library of Congress Cataloging in Publication Data
Holman, Felice.
   The murderer.
   SUMMARY: A young Jewish boy encounters numerous
problems growing up during the Depression in a
Pennsylvania mining town.
   [1. Jews in the United States—Fiction.
2. Pennsylvania—Fiction] I. Title.
PZ7.H7325Mu   [Fic]   78-14266
ISBN 0-684-15904-X

For

HERBERT,

who explained the way things were

and for

JULES,

who knew a lot of answers

He that despiseth his neighbor
lacketh understanding;
But a man of discernment holdeth
his peace.

PROVERBS 11:12

I   the murderer   *3*

II   the girl in the window   *19*

III   the paper route   *38*

IV   the way things are   *48*

V   a musician in the family   *60*

VI   the eclipse   *76*

VII   the new one   *84*

VIII   the wager   *95*

IX   thieves and trouble   *114*

X   gifts   *126*

XI   an end/a beginning   *143*

Ashlymine, Pa., 1932

The purple and green bruise on Hershy Marks's forehead is from an ambush just yesterday. The gash on his nose is healing well and goes back to last week. The rip in his sweater is from a set-to in the schoolyard the other day. Hershy doesn't like to blame God but secretly wonders if He really was paying attention when He plunked him down in Ashlymine, Pennsylvania, but failed to make him Polish.

I

the murderer

HERSHY MARKS found out a long time ago that if he takes a rubber ball and places it very gently near the top of Market Street Hill, opposite his father's hardware store, he can beat it down the hill, running at top speed, though it's a close race. He has to make some adjustments and allowances every year because the settling of the coal mines below heaves the roadway in slightly different places, but usually he can bet on it. Hershy, a first-class sprinter, finds this the most interesting way to get to the bottom of the steep hill.

It might look crazy to someone standing on the square at the top of the hill in Ashlymine, Pennsylvania, that the town is built clinging sideways to the hillside, while at the very bottom are the things a town should cluster about—the Susquehanna River, a slender muddy flow, and the Lackawanna Railroad. Yet the town thins as it nears the river and the railroad seems, from the top of the hill, to be a ladder stretching towards a gray horizon.

The Susquehanna, now looking like a placid stream, is playing 'possum. Almost every spring the river floods, the railroad lies a few inches or even a foot or two under water, and muddy waves lap at the porch steps of the houses down there on First Street. Eleven months of the year the bottom of the hill is dry and great for ball fields. It is that month of the flood that makes the land good for nothing else. And that is why Hershy Marks and the rest of the boys of Ashlymine spend so much time at the bottom of the hill. They think of it as their property, and were upset when the newspapers mentioned building a dike and filling the land. But in the Depression there is no money for that anyway.

Hershy's team is always the last on the field, so that they have to take the marshiest diamond. They are last because they are the boys who have to go to *cheder,* the Hebrew religious school, after public school is through for the day. Then they have to rush to get in their team practice before supper. The other teams have a good edge. They have the dry diamonds, extra practice hours, and many more players. Considering how few Jewish families live in

Ashlymine—just The Hardware, The Jeweler, The Dry Goods, The Variety Store, The Furniture, The Drugstore, The Candy Store, The Meat Market, The Huckster, The Cigar Store, and half a dozen others—it is considered lucky that there are enough boys for a team.

Hershy's team is called the Lions, but through some mistake their shirts came with pictures of tigers on them. Nobody seemed to know what to do about it. Hershy thought it might be possible to rename the team the Tigers, but he has never mentioned it because he figures if it were a good idea someone else would think of it, too.

The other teams are all Polish boys. The best team is the Patriots and is captained by Lorsh Jabieski, son of one of the mine foremen. A blond giant of thirteen, he is, in the mind of Hershy Marks, like a legendary hero mounted on horseback and followed by troops of foot soldiers.

Sometimes when Hershy lies awake in the room over the hardware store which he shares with his small brother, Max, he pretends he is Lorsh, tall and blond, captain of the Patriots, son of a mine foreman, leader of boys and men, and member of that marvelous group of humans, the Poles of Poland and Pennsylvania.

When he plays outfield for the Lions, Hershy is sometimes guilty of missing a fly ball that all but falls into his glove while he gazes across the field to where

Lorsh is pitching to a Patriot batter, winding up with much grace and skill and finishing in a special Lorsh-like curve.

"Catch it, ya dreamin' bum!" Morty Wise yells to Hershy from the Lions' mound. "Ya wanna be onna team or not?" And Hershy ruefully takes after the ball over the marshy ground in the splendid sprint that the Lions expect of him, wipes the ball on his trousers, and heaves it over to Sheldon Appleman at second base. The ball cuts an uneven path through the air, its wrappings flying, its patches hanging loose. Equipment is a constant problem. No one on the team owns a good ball except Lenny Gorin, but the Lions can't rely on him. If Lenny doesn't like a call on a play, he may pick up the ball and go home. Then the game is over. So mostly the Lions play with patched-up equipment, a taped-up ball, split bat, torn gloves. The Patriots have a good ball and bat because the Gregory Coal Company sponsors them. They get their shirts that way, too. On the back they say "Gregory Mines." Once Mr. Marks gave the Lions a new ball, but Hershy hasn't asked for one recently because business is so slow.

It is easy to see the many disadvantages of not being Polish in Ashlymine, quite apart from the marshy diamond. In Ashlymine if you are not from Poland or born of Polish parents, you are a foreigner. Pulaski Day, celebrating the Polish hero who fought with George Washington, is the biggest holiday in the year and the Polish flag is flown above the American flag on the courthouse.

There are only two major occupations in Ashlymine—mining and storekeeping. Though they need each other very much, these two groups are separated in hate by the red ink of the ledger book. If they are to stay in business during the months that the mines are slow or not working, the storekeepers have to give the miners credit, and buying on credit puts the miners into debt even before they dig their wages out of the mine. As if to make this conflict more convenient, the miners are all Polish and the merchants are all Jewish.

Hershy Marks has some complaints of his own. Of all things, it is most unfair that Sunday seems to belong to the Poles. At the Marks house, Sunday is no day at all. While his father sits at the dining table doing accounts and his mother plays solitaire, Hershy crouches in the window over the shop and watches the Poles emerge from Company Street into Market on the way to church. Marvelously cleansed of coal dust, with blue scars from the mines brilliant badges against scrubbed skin, the miners are transformed and beautiful in the sunshine of this, their extra day. Hershy has heard from some of the boys that they are given a special kind of bread by the priest, which is the reason they are so strong and able to beat up their enemies at school when they feel like some fun. This is a lunch hour pastime.

In the bad weather lunch is a dismal hour spent in the classroom, the smell of peanut butter and garlic making the air—already heavy with chalk dust and body smells—almost unbreathable. But on mild days the students are able to take their lunches outside. They form into small groups along the playground wall and on the two amphitheater-like hills that rise from the cemented yard. The preferred spot is the East Hill, where two starving young maple trees give a bit of shade and an outcropping of rock provides the atmosphere of a country picnic. This spot is automatically taken over by the school elite; other young Poles in the upper grades take positions further down the hill. The West Hill, on which grow prickly patches of coarse grass, is the accustomed place for everyone else.

It is Sheldon Appleman—having stuffed himself with thick slices of soft bread with chicken fat, as he reclines on the dusty West Hill with the rest of the Lions—who first speaks out loud of the injustice of the arrangement.

"How come *they* always have the grass and the shade? Huh?"

Every Lion knows the reason, if not in words, at least in its general sense: That's the way things are.

Hershy looks out over the playground and up onto the East Hill where Lorsh lies on the grass, his followers sprawled in idyllic comfort around him. Sheldon, apparently very interested in his own question, closes his eyes as though inviting a trance and speaks slowly.

"Tomorrow I'm going to get out there early and go onto that hill and take that spot."

Morty Wise snorts and Sheldon opens his eyes. Perversely, Sheldon is encouraged. He continues with more animation.

"I'm gonna have to go to the toilet just before lunch, see. Then I'll stay in the boys' room till the lunch bell rings. Then, I'll jimmy that little window that opens right onto the hill and beat it out there before those guys are even to the door. Then, when they come up the hill, I'll say . . ." He pauses to consider what he will say, and observing that he now has the attention of the group, he becomes quite dramatic. "I'll say, 'I don't mind if you fellows join me. Have a seat, but don't kick over my thermos, kindly.' "

Most of the Lions roll over laughing, but Hershy Marks stares at the dreamy-eyed Sheldon with the look of a penniless wanderer finding a gold piece.

"I'll go with ya," he says.

"Hey. . . ." Sheldon starts to protest.

Nutty Cohen, considered by all to be the least likely to amount to anything—not only because he is so fat but also because he lacks vitality or skill at anything at all, now comes strangely alive.

"What I would say," he says slowly, beating a tedious tempo in the air with a pointing finger, "what

I would say is, 'We was here first, see, so . . .' " He takes a deep gulp of air. " 'So go jump in the lake. Go jump in the lake,' I'd say." He laughs contentedly.

Lenny Gorin, son of The Drugstore, and normally a realist, finds himself drawn into the fantasy.

"I would say, 'Why d'ya Polacks think you're so big, ha? What's so great about being a miner, ha? My father lets your father have all kinds of stuff from the drugstore on credit when the mine ain't workin'. So what does that make you? Beggars, just minin' beggars.' That's what I'd say." He takes a bite of dill pickle.

Morty Wise takes his mouth away from his thermos, wipes his lips on his sleeve, and runs his tongue around his teeth.

"I would like to bet a dime none of you wise guys even got the nerve to say one word to big Lorsh, let alone make a smart-aleck speech. I bet a dime. A dime each!"

Sheldon abandons his dream and looks up with interest. Money has a stimulating effect on him. Morty Wise is the one boy who just might be able to back up a bet like that.

"Let's see your money," he says.

Morty reaches into his pocket and draws out a half-dollar. "It'd be worth it," he says. "It'd really be worth it."

"Okay. Who's goin' with me?" Sheldon asks, sitting up.

"I'm goin'," Hershy says.

"Come on, Nutty, with your big mouth. You tell 'em to go jump in the lake," says Sheldon. "How about it, Lenny? Ya yella?"

"I'm not yella," Lenny says.

"I'm not yella," says Nutty.

Just before noon Thursday, Sheldon Appleman raises his hand, looking first over one shoulder at Nutty and Hershy and then over the other shoulder at Lenny.

"Yes, Sheldon?" Miss Holt asks.

"May I be excused?"

"It's five minutes until lunch."

"I got a stomachache," Sheldon says, fixing his face in an expression of controlled pain. The class snickers.

"All right, go," the teacher says. "But hurry back."

Sheldon hurries to the door, then races quickly down two flights of stairs to the basement. Using a ruler he's brought with him, he opens the window that gives directly onto the East Hill. After the bell rings, he is joined by Hershy, Nutty, and Lenny. They are through the window and onto the hill before the rest of the school, not driven by a crusade, is even out on the playground.

Lenny lingers by the window as the others start up the hill to the maple trees.

"This is crazy, Shel. Let's not do it. Morty can keep his lousy dime."

"Ya yella," says Sheldon.

"I'm not yella. I'm smart."

"Ya yella!"

"Ah-h-h." Lenny turns his back on the others and starts towards the playground.

Sheldon looks at Hershy and Nutty. "Come on, we don't need him."

They hurry up the grassy slope, look nervously around as if for an ambush, and then huddle in a close group near the rocks. The only one to open his lunch is Nutty. He is biting into his sandwich with confidence and appetite when Sheldon hisses, "Here they come!"

Up the hill from the playground come ten strapping sons of Poland with their acknowledged king leading them against the slight breeze blowing down the hill. Hershy forgets his nervousness for a moment as he watches his hero and his foot soldiers striding to take the mountain, looking like a picture that he remembers seeing in a book. Suddenly a boy named Georgie, Lorsh's first in command, starts to run towards them.

"Whatcha doin' here, Jews?" he yells.

Sheldon stands up, and Nutty, swallowing his bite of sandwich, stands a second later. The other Patriots are striding faster and, as Sheldon suddenly

hisses, "Let's go!" Georgie and two other Lorsh lieu-
tenants make a lunge for them. Sheldon and Nutty
have an ample start but Hershy, held for a moment
longer by the vision of the King of the Mountain,
is standing as if enchanted when Georgie grabs
him.

"I gotcha, ya smart *Zydek*. Whatcha doin' on the
East Hill? Whatcha doin' in a Christian country, ya
Christ killer?" Georgie shakes Hershy by the arm
which he is holding in his great paw. But Hershy is
staring past Georgie to Lorsh.

"I'm not a Christ killer," he says.

"You're a murderer!" yells Georgie.

"I'm not a murderer." Hershy looks up at the
ruddy face, feeling that perhaps he is to be tortured
on this hill at the hands of a mob. He draws in his
breath and feels a sob gathering in his throat.

Lorsh steps up and puts his hand out. "Let go of
him," he says to Georgie. "Whatcha doin' here?" he
asks with conversational interest.

Hershy looks at him. There is a faint blond fuzz
on Lorsh's upper lip. It glows in the sun. There is
golden hair on his arms. Enormous and blond, he
makes Hershy feel not small and dark, but somehow
bigger and brighter for being near him.

"We thought . . . we thought . . ." he starts.

"Yeah."

"Lemme kill the Christ killer!" says Georgie, flexing his arm.

Lorsh ignores him. "Yeah?"

"We thought it would be nice to eat near the trees. That's all."

"Nobody eats here except us," says Lorsh. "Nobody eats here except us and who we say can eat here."

"I know."

"C'mon Lorsh, lemme beat him up. We don't beat him up a little, they'll try it again."

"Wait a minute," Lorsh says. "I'll take care of him." He comes closer to Hershy and puts his arm out. Hershy flinches, but the arm comes down firmly and without harm on his shoulder. Lorsh leans down to him and speaks intimately. "You are a Christ killer, ya know."

"No," Hershy says. "No, I never killed anyone."

"Yes," Lorsh says, almost sadly. "Yes, ya killed Jesus. Ya can't eat here with us."

Hershy looks up. "Is that why?" he asks.

Lorsh considers a moment. "Yeah, that's why."

"I'm sorry," says Hershy.

"Ya sorry ya killed Christ?"

"No, no! I'm sorry I can't eat with ya. I . . . I like ya."

Lorsh stares at him. Hershy thinks it is a kind look. The look of a kind king. Then Lorsh says slowly, "I tell ya what. Admit ya killed Christ and I'll let ya eat with us today."

"No," Hershy says. "No, I can't."

Georgie is flexing his arm again. "C'mon Lorsh. We're wastin' the whole lunch hour."

"Admit it!" Lorsh says urgently. "Admit it. Ya killed Him."

"No."

"Then get outta here," yells Lorsh. "Get outta here before Georgie beats ya up and don't ever set foot on this hill again if ya wanna live."

Hershy turns away. His lunch bag is over by the rock. He leaves it there.

On the West Hill Hershy is greeted with unaccustomed attention.

"What'd ya say to him?"

"What'd he say to ya?"

"Dint he even beat ya?"

Hershy shrugs. He sits down and stares at his shoes. "They said . . . they only said I killed Christ."

Morty laughs. "Is that all!"

"Why?" Hershy asks. "Why do they say it?"

"Because that's what they think," Morty says.

"But listen," Hershy goes on. "Listen. It isn't true, is it?"

Morty laughs again, but Lenny says, "I once asked the old rabbi and he gave me a big hit on the knuckles with that ruler of his."

"I asked my father once," Sheldon offers.

"What'd he say?" Hershy asks.

"He said, 'Be quiet and take out the garbage!' "

As Hershy comes up the backstairs after Hebrew school and baseball practice, he can hear his mother intoning what amounts to her evening song. The cadences are so familiar. The key words are, "day in, day out," "nearly out of my mind," "worry myself to death." His father listens patiently as though hearing it for the first time. Hershy opens the door to the kitchen. There is a great deal of activity and motion. Pot lids clatter above their steaming contents, plates flash from cupboard to table. His mother is here, there, everywhere.

"Look who's home at last!" She works this into her dirge as if it were the last line of a verse. "Wash up at the sink and sit down to supper. It's nearly cold. What's the matter you don't say anything?" she probes, when he has seated himself at the table. "No hello? Nothing? Max!" she bellows to her younger son. "The soup is on the table. Come!"

Hershy turns to his father. "Pop?"

"Yes?"

"Pop, could I ask you something?"

"Sure. Sure, ask me anything, especially if it's arithmetic." He straightens up and gives Hershy his full attention.

Hershy lowers his voice. "Pop, it isn't true we killed Christ, is it?"

His father looks as though he has not quite understood the question. Then he sits up straighter and begins to open his mouth, but Mrs. Marks slips a plate of soup in front of each of them.

"Eat!" she commands. "For heaven's sake, don't talk. It shouldn't be cold."

His father is peering deeply into the soup, seeming to count the noodles. Does his mother, Hershy wonders, as he studies her closely, look guilty?

When supper is over, Hershy goes to the stairway that leads down into the store. At the turn of the stairs is the phone that serves the store and the house. He sits quietly on the landing, brooding in a cloud of cooking odors which floats down the stairwell and aromas of warm rubber and metal which waft up from the shop.

Will Lorsh have a telephone? Perhaps, since his father is a foreman. Hershy reaches for the phone, hesitates, then speaks softly to the operator.

"Gimme Jabieski," he says. "Jabieski in Company Street." There is a pause and a buzz.

"Hello," someone says.

"I wanna speak to Lorsh."

"To Lorsh!"

"Yeah."

"Okay. Wait."

Hershy waits nervously. He thinks of hanging up. All of a sudden the closeness and the smells in the closed stairwell make him feel a little sick. He swallows hard.

"Hello?"

"Lorsh?"

"Yeah."

"This is Hershy. Hershy Marks."

"Oh. Yeah."

"I just called to tell ya, Lorsh . . ."

"Yeah?"

"I . . . maybe I killed him."

There is no sound for a moment and then, "Atta boy!" Lorsh says. "Atta boy!"

Hershy waits and then when it appears that Lorsh is not going to say any more, he asks very softly, "How about the . . . ya know . . . the eating?"

"What d'ya mean, eating?"

"About me eating on the East Hill, like ya said, ya know?"

"Oh. Well. I'll tell ya. I'll let ya know. Okay?"

"Okay." Hershy hangs up.

He goes upstairs and stands in the half-darkness of the hallway, peering into the mirror. Even allowing for the dim light and poor glass, Hershy thinks the face, still streaked with dust from the ball game, is not as he has imagined the face of a murderer.

It suddenly occurs to him that Morty Wise owes him ten cents.

II

the girl in the window

THE DOORS of the Family Theater in Ashlymine are covered with posters which show a man holding a woman by the throat and bending her backwards, her face fixed in horror. Large standing signs announce coming attractions—*One Hundred Paris Nights, The Eye of Evil.* Neither Hershy Marks nor Sheldon Appleman are allowed to go there. Threats of black-and-blue lickings and a week without dinner (a threat Hershy really doubts his mother would carry out) and other warnings, vague but ominous, keep them away from the attractive doors. They go, instead, to the State Theater where you really get your money's worth—a feature, a travelogue, and a serial—all for a dime, and seen twice if you want.

The theater isn't crowded this Saturday afternoon because the mines are still idle and few people are wasting a good dime on a movie. Besides, the weather is still cold in the early spring and lots of kids are out on the slag heaps picking through mine waste for pieces of coal for the stoves at home. Hershy's mother says the miners' kids have to do that but the Marks family isn't in that condition yet, even though the Depression is making things tough for everyone. "You eat your vegetables and don't waste food and you won't have to climb on any slag heap," she has told him with the kind of logic Hershy is used to. The "Starving Children" is more of the same argument. "You leave lima beans on your plate with the world full of Poor Starving Children!" Mrs. Marks sometimes gasps in horror. Then guilt floods Hershy as he chokes down the big watery white beans, apparently saving many poor children as he does so.

Although, as the son of one of the town's merchants, he enjoys some of his differences from the miners' kids—the storekeepers are just better off—in general, he would prefer to be more like them, if only because there are so many of them. However, the slag heap is not one of the places he is anxious to join them. Nearly every month the newspapers, which Hershy reads daily, report yet another awful accident on the slag—a slide, a cave-in.

The show begins with the *Movietone News*. It is at least a week or two behind the news in the daily paper.

LINDBERGH BABY KIDNAPPED.

The famous Lone Eagle, the first man to fly alone across the Atlantic, and his wife are shown in the house where the nurse found the baby missing. They are waiting to hear from the kidnappers.

JAPANESE ROUT CHINESE IN FIERCE SHANGHAI BATTLE.

A war is going on and the Chinese are losing. A truce is expected soon.

ROOSEVELT SET TO BATTLE FOR PRESIDENCY.

This one isn't a war. It is about someone who wants to be the next President of the United States.

Next comes a travelogue of Hawaii. Hershy really enjoys it. He has never seen the ocean except in pictures. It is hard to believe in the palm trees, the lithe men climbing the leaning trunks of coconut trees, the great sweeping surf. The landscape is so expansive compared to the Valley, closed in by hills broken only by the black skeletons of the coal breakers and heaps of black slag. Hershy wonders who gets to go to places like Hawaii. Probably someone who wins a prize for something.

"And now we bid a sad farewell to beautiful Hawaii." And the feature comes on—Greta Garbo and John Barrymore in *Grand Hotel*. Greta Garbo is a dancer and John Barrymore is a baron. Hershy isn't crazy about the movie. He decides he likes the movies in which the action takes place outdoors, mostly. A Tom Mix cowboy movie is best, or else a Tarzan picture. This stuff is mostly indoors and Hershy is pretty embarrassed by Greta Garbo kissing John Barrymore. The way she looks at him! Eeeesh! Hershy kicks the seat in front of him so much that an old lady in the next aisle tells him to quit it. Sheldon is even worse. He hoots and whistles and embarrasses Hershy even more. But finally they get to the end of *Grand Hotel* and see the next reel of a terrific serial, *The Masked Rider*. Hershy has seen all the reels and thinks he knows who the masked rider is. For him, this is the best part of the show.

But he is glad when the movie is over. Coming out into the gray rain-soaked air is a shock to the system. The theater's air had been warmed by being breathed over and over. The hours of darkness have made the eyes sensitive to even the dull afternoon light. Hershy's legs feel stiff.

They walk slowly down Main Street and start kicking their way toward Market Street and the square—a green oasis in the gray town. Hershy has spent many hours of his life running laps around it. But now he hangs back to look in the window of Morris's Jewelry Store.

"Come on, Hersh!" whines Sheldon. "Whatcha wanna look at that stuff for?"

"I dunno," Hershy says. "My mother's birthday is next week and I gotta get her something."

"You're not gonna get her something here," chafes Sheldon. "This stuff must cost a jillion."

"Yeah," Hershy says, "but I wanna give her something nice. I just don't know what."

"How much ya got?"

"Fifty cents, from handing out the advertisements for the Siren Dress Shop."

Sheldon looks impressed. "Yeah, but that's not enough for jools."

"No," Hershy agrees. The matter of the gift is weighing on him heavily. His mother, though she nags him and embarrasses him and generally harasses him, is, after all, his mother, and on her birthday he wants to let her know he understands that she means well.

They are nearly to the corner when they are stopped by a truly fascinating sight. What appears to be a real live grown-up girl with yellow hair is sitting in the window of Stein's Furniture Store. She is seated on a carved chair with red velvet arms in the midst of a bedroom setting. Her back is very straight and her eyes are fixed straight ahead. She wears a satiny dress of bright purple.

"What's she doin' in the window?" asks Sheldon.

Hershy shrugs and peers more closely.

"She wasn't there when I came down the hill this morning," Sheldon says. He examines the girl thoroughly. "I think it's a dummy."

"No, look at her eyelids," says Hershy. "They blink."

"Okay, so what's she doin' there?" Sheldon persists. He does not usually work up this much interest in things that have nothing to do with him. Usually for something to be interesting to Sheldon, a person should be able to use it in some way or at least eat it.

Hershy now moves his gaze from the girl, herself, to a sign that is illuminated by a blinking light.

"It's a stunt," he says, "to get business. Remember last year they had the Human Fly that climbed the bank?"

The sign reads:

SEE THE GORGEOUS GIRL HYPNOTIZED

at noon
all this week
except Sunday

FREE BEDROOM SUITE
TO ANYONE WHO CAN MAKE HER SMILE

A sun is rising in Hershy's heart. "I'm gonna do it!" he yells, hopping around on the sidewalk, splashing his tweed knickers with the blackish film of mud that runs down the walks as the light rain mixes with coal dust.

Sheldon is skeptical. "There's gotta be a catch," he says.

"Be quiet," says Hershy. "I'm gonna try it now." He thinks for a moment, then bends down, grabs his ankles with his hands, and puts his head between his legs so that he is looking backwards. He saw a rubber man doing something like that in a carnival over in Wilkes-Barre once. Then he edges his way back and forth in front of the window.

"Keep your eye on her," he directs Sheldon. The blood runs to his head and the world turns upside down around him.

"She's not moving," Sheldon reports.

Hershy has planned to complete his act by lowering his back to the wet pavement and doing a somersault, but Tom Grabowski and Jim Romanski rush him and push him over hard.

"Ya dumb *Zydek!*" yells Jim.

Hershy picks himself up and calls to Sheldon, who has ducked out of the way, "Did she do anything?"

"Nothin'," Sheldon says.

"I'm gonna do my fish, then," Hershy says, just as the curtains at the back of the window part and a tall man in a black suit comes into the show window and moves towards the chair. He glances briefly at Hershy and Sheldon, then, standing over the girl, he makes some spooky waving motions with his arms. When the man taps the girl on the shoulder, she stretches and rises from the chair.

"He's unhypnotizing her," Sheldon says.

Straightening her skirt, she looks down and grins at Hershy and Sheldon. Then she walks behind the curtain and the man follows. A second later the window goes dark.

"Heck!" says Hershy. "I would've got her with the fish act. I'm comin' back on Monday at lunch hour. Ya comin' with me?"

"Sure," Sheldon says.

Kaiser, the Markses' dog, lies at the bottom of the backstairs getting the last rays of the sun. He does not move and Hershy leaps over him. He has mixed feelings about Kaiser, who is handsome and a good watchdog, a genuine German Shepherd. As a German of good pedigree, the dog is respected by the Polish townspeople. Hershy feels that Kaiser has a more secure place in the community than he does. So, while he is proud of his association with Kaiser, he resents him and is, in fact, envious of his position, of his background and genealogy. No Pole ever lies in wait to knock Kaiser into the gutter or even to pull his tail. No, they stand around the store stroking his lustrous coat. Sometimes this burns Hershy up.

Kaiser at the bottom of the stairs and a strange man at the top—another hobo, Hershy supposes. The stranger is devouring an egg sandwich that Mrs. Marks has given him, washing it down with great gulps of milk. Every day the trains spill some of the Depression's homeless people into the station yard. Sometimes they jump out of the boxcars before the train reaches the station. Hershy has seen them do it many times. Sometimes they are thrown off by the trainmen as they are discovered traveling from town to town, looking for work or a place to sleep and a bite to eat. They hang around, sometimes begging on the street, but more often coming around to the back doors of houses and asking for a handout. Mrs. Marks has never turned anyone away. She gives them leftovers or a sandwich. On the other hand, she never lets them in, no matter what the weather.

"They tell you they used to be businessmen," she says. "They tell you they owned real estate or that they were college students. But who knows, with the riffraff they associate with in those boxcars, what they may be now. You can't take chances."

Why come to Ashlymine? Hershy wonders. The people here don't have much to give. He guesses the hoboes don't know that until they get here. This one, Mrs. Marks says, is not a hobo but a miner from way over the other side of Nanticoke. He hasn't worked in six months. He got hurt in a mine explosion and can't move his right arm. Mrs. Marks is packing a small bag with boiled eggs and bread for him to take to his children. "They beg where nobody knows them," she says.

"I wonder if that miner knows this is a Jewish house?" Hershy asks. "D'ya think a Polack wants to take a handout from Jews?"

Mr. Marks has come into the kitchen. "There's no Hebrew word for that kind of charity," he says. "The Talmud says we must give to the poor, be he Jew or Gentile."

Now Mrs. Marks focuses on Hershy. "What did you do, roll all the way home?" she asks, looking over his sweater and pants. "Maybe you were sweeping the streets with your clothes? What's the use giving you good things to wear if you go in the mud with them? You look like a hobo yourself."

The sulphuric odor of hard-boiled eggs plus the harangue about his clothes dampens Hershy's enthusiasm for the bedroom suite for a little while. However, it is rekindled at supper by a dessert of cold bread pudding full of raisins.

Monday. Lunch hour. Hershy and Sheldon eat their peanut butter sandwiches on the run and arrive at Stein's Furniture Store in time to join a sprinkling of people watching the hypnotizing. There isn't much shopping going on in town these days. People have no money to spend, since the mines are working only two days a week. A light gray rain is still falling, and this also discourages standing around.

The curtain parts and the man in black and the yellow-haired girl come out and bow. Then the girl sits down and the man makes the same waving motions over her that he did Saturday afternoon when he unhypnotized her. Then he makes a sort of whammy motion, at which point she starts to stare ahead just as she had on Saturday. After that the man backs out of the window and several people in the crowd begin to make funny faces, hammer on the window, and crack jokes, which, Hershy figures, she probably can't hear.

Hershy is nervous. What if one of them makes her smile before he has a chance to try? People come and go during the entire lunch hour and the girl doesn't change her expression.

"Do it if you're gonna do it," Sheldon urges. "We gotta get back to school."

"Not with all these people around," Hershy says. "I'm waitin' for them to go back to work."

Hershy and Sheldon duck in and out among the spectators, watching the various halfhearted attempts to make the girl laugh. But that, Hershy decides, is the trouble: Nobody is really trying.

The janitor of the store is sweeping wet coal dust out to the curb. "Come on, Hersh," Sheldon urges. "There's just this one goop and he's not watchin' ya."

"Okay," Hershy says, taking his stand directly in front of the girl. "Here goes the fish."

He draws in his breath and then, exhaling through his nose, puffs out his cheeks enormously. When they are fully extended, he crosses his eyes. This is an act of total sacrifice because when he performs he can't see a thing, nor, for some reason, can he hear very well. He holds the fish face for the count of forty-five and then draws in his breath, deflates his cheeks, and straightens his eyes. The fish face is a never-fail act in the classroom when the teacher is out of the room for a few minutes and Hershy can rely on it to bring down the house.

"She didn't fall for it," Sheldon says.

"Were ya watchin' her every second?"

"You know me," Sheldon says. "If I say I'm gonna do somethin', I do it, don't I? I didn't take my eyes off her."

"Okay, I'm gonna do it again," Hershy says. "Better."

He inhales and exhales a few times to exercise his lungs, then places himself a little further from the window, directly in the girl's gaze. He inhales again and then, blowing the air into his cheeks, stretches them until they nearly burst. Then he crosses his eyes until fuzzy light is all he can see. He counts thirty, forty, fifty, sixty, seventy . . .

Then he is looking up at the gray sky and Sheldon and the janitor are leaning over him. Sheldon is yelling, "Hershy, hey Hershy!" His head hurts.

The janitor says, "You passed out."

"Ya crazy?" yells Sheldon.

Hershy feels like throwing up.

"Did she smile?" is the first thing he says when he can talk.

"Nope," Sheldon says. "And I bet she's not gonna."

Hershy sits up holding his head, and stares into the window. He could swear the girl's eyes have moved from the place they had been fixed on. He thinks her hand may have moved a little. Sheldon doesn't think so.

"Listen," says Hershy, now recovered except for a bump, his mind racing on a new tack. "What pieces of furniture are in this bedroom suite? Let's see. A wardrobe. We don't need that. We have a closet. I tell ya what I'll do. I'll give ya the wardrobe for your mother if ya help me."

"I dunno," Sheldon says. "Is that fair? You get everything and I just get the wardrobe. Anyway, what do I have to do?"

"All right," Hershy says. "I'll give ya the bedside stand, too. How about that? It's fair because I'm gonna do most everything. You just have to help a little."

"Okay, okay," says Sheldon.

"Promise!" Hershy demands. "I gotta rely on ya because I gotta get this present. It's urgent."

"All right, all right. I promise," Sheldon swears.

"Okay then. Meet me here right after *cheder*. I have to stop off at my house and pick up somethin', but I'll be here at four-thirty on the dot. You be here. Okay?"

"Okay, okay. Now hurry up or we're gonna be late."

In *cheder*, the old rabbi sits at his desk in front of the classroom. In his dusty black suit and his black *yarmulke* he looks, Hershy thinks, like a skinny blackbird up at Newbury Knob, the craggy hill where the boys like to climb. His bright eyes hooded with wrinkled lids, his face sharp, his hands gnarled into claws by arthritis. Something has happened to his voice over the years and it now comes out strangled and thin instead of big and strong as it used to. He looks

pained and hunched in this, his last year, at the *shul*.
He is too old to carry on. What happens to old rabbis? Hershy wonders.

Some of the older boys, and boys now men, have
tales to tell about the old rabbi. He had been a
famous hitter. The ruler was a wicked weapon in his
hand, landing on knuckles, heads, and backs when
students irked him with mischief or undone lessons.
But in recent years his will seems to have become as
weak as his arms and voice. The ruler lies inactive on
his desk. The lessons move slowly, maddeningly
slowly for Hershy who fears someone will get down
to Stein's and make the girl smile before he does.

Rabbi Aaron is reading a lesson on ethics, stopping after each sentence to have the boys repeat the
difficult Hebrew sounds after him, as they follow in
their books. One of the rabbi's crooked fingers
points to his place in the old book, his other hand
stiffly leads the unison voices.

"Again," says Rabbi Aaron. "Repeat."

Hershy intones the dirge with the rest of the
class. He can't pay attention. His eyes stray to the
English translation on the lefthand page: "Be forward to all men, and be rather as the tail of the lion
than the head of the fox."

He would like to ask the rabbi what that means.
It could mean that the lion is brave, so be like the
lion. And the fox is . . . is sneaky, so don't be like
the fox. But why the tail? Why the head? Maybe
because the tail follows the head of the courageous

lion. Or maybe, *maybe* the head is where the teeth are and the tail is more friendly. Why did the old rabbis who wrote this stuff talk that way? Why didn't they just talk straight? So we could all sit here thousands of years later and say it over and over like this?

Come on, come on! Hershy thinks. Finish up! I *gotta* get out of here!

Hershy runs like a fox, he thinks, or even like a fox pursued by a lion. He tears down Kosciusko Street, around into Market, up the stairs, through the store, and into the house. He dashes into a bedroom, a broom closet, a storeroom, stuffing things into a bag. Then down the stairs, out of the store, and down the street to Stein's. Even so, he is there before Sheldon. Where *is* he?

Hershy is relieved to see the girl still in the window. He thinks that by now probably everyone in town must know about and have tried his luck at amusing the girl. There doesn't seem to be much interest among the few passers-by. A casual glance and a face made in passing is all, as people hurry home at the end of the damp day. Hershy has been stamping impatiently around in the black rain for five minutes when Sheldon arrives on the run.

"Heck, Sheldon! It's almost closin' time. You're supposed to be so reliable."

"Well, I'm here now," Sheldon says. "I got tangled up with that Jim Romanski. I wish he'd pick on someone else for a while."

"Okay," Hershy says, recognizing a valid excuse. He reaches into the large paper bag he carries. "You put this on," and he hands Sheldon a long tailcoat that Mr. Marks had worn at his wedding and probably never since.

"Put that on? Ya crazy! Why should I put that on?"

"Because ya promised. Unless you're gonna break a solemn promise, of course."

"Okay, okay," Sheldon mutters. "But wait until there's nobody else around. What're ya gonna put on?"

"This," Hershy says, and he pulls from the bag a long flowered skirt of his mother's which he slips over his pants, and an orangey mophead which he plops over his hair.

"What d'ya think you're doin'!" cries Sheldon.

"Just shut up and come on over here and do what I say."

Hershy plants himself in front of the window, looking right and left to be sure nobody is paying attention. There is a lull on Market Street. Then Hershy falls to his knees in front of Sheldon and grabs him about the waist.

"Don't go! Don't go!" Hershy cries in a voice much higher than his normal one.

"Don't go where?" asks Sheldon.

"Just be quiet," Hershy whispers. "Pat me on the head and stroke my hair. Come on. *Do it!*"

With a hand held like a frozen mitten at the end

of a stiffened arm, Sheldon pats and strokes the mop on Hershy's head.

"Don't go! Don't go, Baron!" Hershy cries, and then he raises his face and slowly, using Sheldon as a climbing pole, pulls himself up until they are face to face. Then he suddenly throws his arms around Sheldon, who is struggling to keep his balance, and gives him a walloping kiss.

Sheldon lets out a yowl that can be heard up and down Market Street and around on Main. A ribbon of abuse unrolls from his tongue. Tears threaten his eyes. "I'll never talk to you again, you . . . you . . ."

But Hershy isn't listening. His attention has immediately turned to the girl in the window. No question about it, she is struggling to keep from laughing out loud.

"I did it! We did it! Sheldon, she's smiling."

Sheldon tears off the tailcoat and throws it at Hershy. Then he turns and stamps down the street.

"Come on back. We gotta claim the prize," yells Hershy. Sheldon doesn't turn around.

Hershy takes off his wig and skirt and stuffs them and the tailcoat into the paper bag. Then he goes into the store.

"I wanna see Mr. Stein," he says to the clerk.

"What about?"

"About the bedroom suite."

"What bedroom suite?"

"You know. The suite I get for makin' the girl laugh."

"What's all this?" a voice calls from the back.

"There's a boy here says he made Anna laugh," says the clerk.

"Yeah? Let me see him." Mr. Stein waddles out of the stockroom, ducking his big round stomach over and under pieces of furniture as he walks.

"Well, aren't you the Marks boy? How are you, sonny?"

"I'm fine, Mr. Stein. Me and Sheldon Appleman just made the girl laugh."

"Hoo ha! Says you! Who saw you do it?"

"Sheldon. He saw me."

"Who else?"

"Nobody else. Nobody was around."

"You got no witnesses!"

A terrible feeling begins to build up in Hershy. "It didn't say we needed witnesses."

"Now, you look like a bright boy. Aren't you the kid who won the essay contest in the *Wilkes-Barre Record?*" Hershy nods. It is one of his proudest accomplishments to have had something he wrote printed in the newspapers.

"Well then, think. Do you expect me to give away a bedroom suite to anyone who comes in here and says he made her laugh? Do you? Be reasonable."

Hershy is feeling desperate. Wild. "But I *did* it!" he yells.

"Hey, hey! No yelling around here."

"Ask her. Go ahead. Ask her." Hershy pulls away the curtain behind him.

"Now look here, you ruffian!" But Hershy is already standing in the window entreating the girl.

"Go ahead, tell him. Tell him ya smiled." She does not blink.

"Out!" yells Mr. Stein. "Out of my window and out of my store. And if you make any more rowdy stuff I'm going to complain to your father."

"Please," Hershy whispers to the girl as he backs out of the window. "Tell him!"

Mr. Stein has Hershy by the collar and headed for the door.

"She's got crooked teeth," yells Hershy, as the door closes. "Doesn't that prove it? She's got crooked teeth. I saw them."

Standing on the wet street in front of Stein's, Hershy looks daggers at the girl. He stands and scowls at her for several minutes, brooding. Then he picks up his bag and starts down Market Street, shaking his head.

He stands for a while, thinking, in front of a shabby little store at the corner of Main, then he slowly opens the door and walks in. He paces up and down in front of the counter. After long consideration he selects from a tray of assorted objects a heart-shaped brooch carved of polished coal, pays fifty cents for it, and takes it home. It isn't what he had in mind at all.

III

the paper route

HERSHY FINDS he is able to make the sun rise. As he walks up the steep incline of Market Street very early in the morning, and the sun is still below the distant hills, there is a certain point where he can stop, stand back on his heels, and then rise slowly on his toes to make the sun appear. The interesting part is that this point is a little different every day.

The sun that rises over the mountains to light Ashlymine has been somewhere else before—New York, China even. But life beyond the hills is only a myth because, from the Valley, the wall of mountains and black slag seems to be the perimeter of the world. Even when Hershy climbs the rocky and wooded hill to Newbury Knob and looks beyond, he sees only more of the same. And yet he knows there is life beyond the wall. The newsreels tell of this almost mythical life in which entirely different kinds of people do entirely different kinds of things.

A bundle of newspapers is slung over Hershy's shoulder. Morty's younger brother, Milt, has the paper route but he has the chicken pox and Hershy has agreed to distribute the papers until he's okay again. Though Hershy has to get up in the dark to do it, he is glad to earn the money. As yet, he isn't familiar with the route and has to keep referring to the list of subscribers to the *Wilkes-Barre Record*. Sometimes there is quite a walk between houses. Lots of people, if they take a paper at all, take the *Ashly-mine News* in the afternoon because that's where they find out the news they really want to know—which mines will be open the next day.

"Yer late," an old man growls as Hershy approaches. Early as it is, the man has been waiting on his porch for the paper. Hershy hands it to him and the old man squints at him. "Yer not the same boy," he complains.

"No, Milty's sick."

"Don't be so late tomorrow," the old man says. A dog barks loudly as the man opens his door to go in, and from the depths of the house wafts the heavy smell of boiled coffee.

Hershy moves on and starts to fold a paper for the next porch and, as he does, he sees a headline on the fold that strikes him as very strange.

GERMANY FOR THE GERMANS
SAYS ADOLF HITLER

Who else would it be for! He reads a little more. "To achieve German liberation," Hitler says, "it is necessary to defeat the enemies of Germany—the Communists and the Jews." *And the Jews!* So! It is not just in Ashlymine that there is trouble. Hershy sits on the running board of a Ford parked on the street and reads on. It seems that the Germans are going to elect a President tomorrow. Nobody knows if the man named Hindenburg, who is President now, will win because this Hitler has a lot of people who are for him. Besides that he has a bunch of storm troopers, a sort of private army. But it doesn't say any more about what Hitler wants to do to defeat the enemies of Germany. Hershy hopes Hitler will lose.

He has to rush to finish the route and is late for school anyway. He is sent down to Mr. Kowalski, the principal. When Mr. Kowalski hears the excuse—the paper route Hershy is taking over for poor sick Milty—he lets Hershy off with one day of detention.

"But I can't stay after school," Hershy protests. "I have to go to *cheder.*"

Mr. Kowalski scowls. "Then come down here in your study hour and just sit," he says.

Hershy does that, but he thinks it's silly. What good is he doing sitting on a bench in the principal's office?

He sits on the hard bench with the regular truants and mischief-makers, who Mr. Kowalski likes to keep an eye on.

"Whadya know!" whispers Jim Romanski. "One of God's Chosen People is down here with the rest of us. Now how could a thing like that happen!"

Even the rabbi says they are God's Chosen People. But Hershy thinks, if this is true, it is more trouble to be chosen than not to be.

"Ya know what they been chosen for?" Jim asks his fellow Poles. "To get their peckers cut off."

"Shut up out there," yells Mr. Kowalski.

It's the same old story. Even in the boys' room there is no sanctuary. Just like Jim did now, they poke fun at him and the other Jewish boys. When he goes to the urinal, Hershy tries to hide the part that announces that every bit of him is different.

It is only eleven o'clock but it has been a long day.

In the late afternoon his father stops him on his way through the store into the house.

"Would you give me a hand, Hershy?" His father is always apologetic when he asks for help. It makes Hershy feel guilty. Perhaps he should offer more. He is willing, but most of the time things are so slow that there isn't much to do and he forgets.

"Sure," he says.

"I need two dozen glasses wrapped for Mrs. Green. She's having a party for the sister-in-law from Pittsburgh. Would you mind going down to the basement and wrapping some for me? I don't want to leave the store."

"But I just unwrapped 'em!"

"I know. But these days who would think anyone would be buying two dozen glasses?"

Hershy drops his books and goes down the wooden cellar stairs, holding onto the rail that runs along the cracked damp wall. He hates the cellar. He feels he is only a hair's breadth from the mine as, in fact, he is. He thinks that right beneath him bent-backed, smudge-faced, wet, cold men are hacking away at the hard black walls. He imagines that he can hear their picks. The cellar is stacked with crates, mostly empty, and some excess merchandise, barrels of nails, and rolls of wire screening. Hershy seats himself on an empty crate near the stack of glasses and begins wrapping them in paper. There is a pile of old newspapers near at hand and first he stuffs a glass with a piece and then very carefully rolls it up, on the bias, in another.

He has wrapped three when the light from the bare bulb over his head illuminates a headline on the page he is about to wrap around the glass.

LINDBERGH PICKS UNDERWORLD
GO-BETWEENS IN ATTEMPT TO
REACH KIDNAPPERS

What is happening is that Lindbergh is trying all kinds of ways to get in touch with the people who have taken his son. But so far nothing has happened. This is a terribly sad story and everyone in the country is all upset, but it is also very interesting—like a Nick Carter book, the detective series that Hershy likes to read.

On the same page there is more about Hitler and the German election. The paper says that the election is important not only for Germany but for the whole world. How come? The paper answers Hershy's question right away. Because, it says, it will decide the future of Fascism and even Communism. Hershy doesn't understand all this exactly, but what interests him is that something going on in Germany could be important to everyone, which means him, too, here in Ashlymine. What he really wants to know is how the election turns out. Will that old guy, President Hindenburg, win, or will this younger guy, Hitler, who looks a lot like Charlie Chaplin but with straight hair, and who wants to defeat the Jews?

He wraps three more glasses, now peeking to see what story he is wrapping around each glass. He has just wrapped one in a headline about the American elections:

ROOSEVELT LEADS IN PRIMARY

Another really interesting story is about a trolley holdup right in Wilkes-Barre. Some thieves jumped onto the rear of a car and when it reached a lonely spot, they pulled the trolley from the wire and held up the driver and the passengers.

"Hershy, are you finished?"

"Yeah, just about." For once, he hasn't really minded working in the cellar.

When he comes upstairs with the glasses, he announces a fact he has just discovered in one of the little stories at the bottom of a page. "Pop, ya know the inside of the sun is twenty-nine million degrees!"

"You don't say! Where did you hear that?"

Hershy shrugs. "In the newspaper."

Halfway up the hill the next morning, he sits down on a stoop to open the paper and find out what happened in the German election.

HINDENBURG WINS

Hershy cheers.

"What's the big racket?" growls the old man with the dog.

"Hitler lost," Hershy says.

"That's no reason to make such a row. My old lady is still asleep."

Hershy reads the rest of the story on his way to the next house. Hindenburg has ordered Hitler to disband his army and stop all the terrorizing. But Hitler said, "We must march further towards our goal. Our work has just begun."

Hershy forgets to make the sun rise.

On the way to school, after delivering the papers, he sees the old rabbi trying to wrestle a bulky package out of his mailbox. Hershy puts down his books and helps him.

"Thank you, Herschel," the old rabbi says. "I guess these must be the copies of the *Jewish Daily Forward* that my cousin sends me from New York when he is through with them. I'm glad to have them. I just finished the last bunch."

"Isn't the news kind of old when ya get it?" Hershy asks.

"Hey?" The rabbi cups his ear.

Hershy raises his voice. "I say, isn't the news all over and done with when ya get to read it?"

The rabbi nods, closes his eyes, nods some more, and smiles patiently. "Herschel," he says. "What difference to me if a man got robbed today or yesterday or last week? Do I care, when some politician says something, if he says it now or said it last month?"

Hershy has noticed before that the rabbi usually offers a list of questions before he starts in on the answer.

"Why don't I care? you ask. I'll tell you why I don't care. Because the important things that affect my life and your life, they all happened a couple of thousand years ago before there was a newspaper."

"Like what?" Hershy asks.

"Like Moses led the Children of Israel out of bondage. And the Lord gave him the Ten Commandments. Like the Israelites were driven from their land in the *Diaspora,* the Great Dispersion, and scattered all over the world. Those are the things that have made me what I am, that have brought me to this place. So what does it matter if I hold the paper for today or yesterday or last month?"

Hershy considers this. He can see how the rabbi feels. A day, a month, even a year, is not much in the long line of years of great events. But maybe he's wrong, too. Couldn't some great event happen right now? How would a person know about it if he didn't read it in the newspapers or hear it on the radio or see it in the newsreel? If Moses had just got hold of the Ten Commandments yesterday, wouldn't the rabbi want to know about it right away? Hershy is afraid to ask this. But the mention of the Great Dispersion raises another question in his mind and, since he has the rabbi's attention, he takes advantage of it.

"Rabbi, can I ask you somethin'?"

"Go ahead, Herschel. I still got ears, but you better yell."

"Rabbi, listen. The Poles come from Poland. Right?"

The rabbi raises his eyebrows. "This is a question?"

Hershy hurries on. "And the Irish, they come from Ireland. So, where do the Jews come from?"

"Ai," wails the rabbi. "Where *don't* they come from?" See! Another question. Hershy waits. The answer will probably come.

"Listen, they wandered everywhere. Some came first to Spain and Italy, then to France, to England, to Germany. Then they went to countries in eastern Europe, and later a lot of them came to this place, to America."

"And in Germany, are they the enemies of the Germans?"

"What are you, *meshugge!* Some of the greatest Germans are Jews. You never heard of Einstein? Mendelssohn?"

Hershy nods. "And Poland? Did they go to Poland?"

"Did they go to Poland! Thousands! And thousands of Polish Jews came here. I am, myself, from Poland."

The rabbi is a Polack! Hershy finds this hard to believe.

"But if Jews can also be from Poland, then why can't they be like the Polacks here?"

The rabbi closes his eyes, shakes his head, and rolls his eyes. "Herschel, go! That's enough questions, already." He hesitates, and then he says, "A Jew is a Jew and a Pole is a Pole. Don't say I didn't give you an answer." He turns and goes towards his door.

Hershy kicks the porch railing. Who has the answers?

the way things are

HERSHY MARKS is doing his crab walk up the hill, toes in, elbows turned out. The morning sun, hanging low over the mountain, illuminates this act which only he in the entire valley, country, and perhaps, world, is doing at just this moment.

"Come on, Hershy!" Sheldon urges. "We're gonna be late."

Hershy abandons his crawl. It doesn't matter now. He's already done it. He doesn't explain to Sheldon the feeling of uniqueness and originality that he gets from these brief antic moments—not just the crab walk but anything else different.

A sudden rush behind them and two big blond boys shoulder them into the gutter, grab their books, and toss them into the mud. *"Zydek!"* They spit on the ground as they run past.

"Darn Polacks!" Sheldon mutters, brushing himself off and wiping his books with his handkerchief. "They think they own the streets. Why do they think they can do anything they want to us?"

Hershy picks himself up and shakes his head. It is the way things are. They resume their climb to school, as the great sun now colors the whole gray town gold.

At the top of Kosciusko Street, Hershy and Sheldon turn into the school grounds and come upon a small crowd of Lions gathered in a corner behind the generator shed.

"Ya got fifty movie cards on ya?" Morty calls to them. "Jeanie Green's going to unbutton her blouse for us if we give her fifty cards."

Hershy shakes his head. Jeanie Green's chest may be intriguing, but it sure isn't worth any cards. He feels certain he can get a better deal. As a matter of fact Morty has a couple of cards he'd like to trade for, a Hoot Gibson and a Tim McCoy.

All the same, it makes Hershy think that he hardly ever sees any girls around town except in class. He wonders what happens to them after school. It's like they disappear. Not that he cares. But he just wonders, having no sisters, what girls do while boys are playing ball, running around the

square, or going to *cheder*. He asks Nutty Cohen, one
day, because Nutty has a younger sister.

"Her! She just hangs around makin' dresses for
her paper doll."

"Is that all?"

"Well, she listens to the radio. She likes the Lone
Ranger, and sometimes she goes to the movies on a
Saturday afternoon. Why d'ya wanna know? Ya like
her?"

"No!" Hershy is alarmed. "Why should I like
her? I just wondered what they do."

"That's all they do," Nutty says in his slow voice.
"That's abolutely all they do."

"When do they learn . . . ya know . . . when do
they learn stuff girls know?"

"Like what?" Nutty asks.

"Like how to cook and be . . . like a mother?"
Nutty shrugs. Hershy's face feels hot. He wishes he
hadn't asked all this. There isn't even one girl in
town he even knows is alive, except maybe Lorsh
Jabieski's older sister, Alice, and that's just because
she is Lorsh's sister. But now that he thinks of it, he
wonders what she does in the afternoons. She's in
high school already. He just can't believe that she
dresses dolls. She is tall and smooth skinned and
bright eyed like Lorsh, and she paints her toenails
and puts sprinkles on them like a cupcake. He knows
this because he saw her wading at the creek last summer.

Hershy sits in class and lets his attention wander from Miss Holt, who is reading to them from a book by Mark Twain called *Huckleberry Finn*. Hershy has gotten the book from the library to read himself because he can't stand the suspense of reading the book a chapter every few days. He is way ahead in the story. Now he looks around at the kids in the class. In the back, where he sits, Jim Romanski and Tom Grabowski are slumped in their seats, looking alternately at the ceiling and at each other with pain and boredom. They sit in the back because they are so tall. On the other side, Sheldon sits with his glasses fallen to the end of his nose, leaning forward to catch every word. He likes stories but he doesn't read as much as Hershy because he spends a lot of time drawing maps to go with his geography and history homework. Hershy does his homework on brown paper which he tears evenly from the roll of wrapping paper in the store. It's okay, but it doesn't look as good as Sheldon's, which is on real lined white paper.

In front of Sheldon, Mary Grabowski, Tom's younger sister, draws pictures in her notebook. Hershy wonders how Tom feels about having his younger sister in the same class. Hershy knows he would mind if his little brother, Max, were in his class. It would be embarrassing. Tom never seems to be embarrassed. He's not so dumb. It's just that he misses a lot of school and has been left back. A lot of

the time, in the spring and fall, Tom doesn't come to
school because he has to work on the farm. The
school has tried to make his father send him, but his
father needs him. Hershy wonders what would happen if his father needed him in the store.

Miss Holt keeps the slowest kids and the kids who
pay least attention in the front of the room. Nutty
Cohen sits up front. The rest are mostly blond heads
moving restlessly. Hershy looks at them. He looks
down the aisle at the torn sneakers sticking out from
under desks. The raggedy clothing. He knows that
their lunch bags sometimes contain only hunks of
bread. And these are his enemies? He wants to tell
them he does not hate them, even though they may
hate him and harass him. He wants to tell them he is
sorry they are so poor and that their fathers have no
work.

Tom Grabowski's big foot strays under Hershy's
desk and slams down on his sneakered toes. Hershy
winces and looks straight ahead. He tries to act as if
nothing is happening. Now Tom leans over slowly
and pushes all of Hershy's books to the floor, papers
flying.

Miss Holt looks up. "I'm surprised at you, Herschel," she says with disapproval. "I don't usually expect you to cause the disturbances during the read-
ings. Hurry up! Get those things picked up and get
back to your seat."

Tom and Jim are smug with pleasure. "See,

Zydek! Ya ain't gonna be teacher's pet too long," Tom hisses.

Just because he does his work and knows the answers they like to call him teacher's pet. Ah!

"While you're up, please open the window, Herschel," says Miss Holt.

Hershy goes around the back of the room to the enormous windows, with the sooty glass and gritty sills. He grabs the mud-colored frame and pushes. It doesn't move. He puts his back into it and pushes harder. A rough hand knocks him away from the window. Tom Grabowski, towering six inches over Hershy, pulls the window down from the top.

"How ya gonna get any muscles if ya don't eat pork, ya skinny *Zydek,*" Tom hisses.

Hershy wonders if all his life he is to be humiliated thus or will he suddenly get a foot taller and grow very strong. Look at the way his leg muscles are from all the running. But even so—even if he were bigger and tougher—that wouldn't be the whole story, and he knows it. He wonders if the Poles and the Jews have difficulties in the rest of the country or just in the Valley. Is it the same in New York and in St. Louis? If it isn't, Hershy thinks, sooner or later, he will want to go there. But how? What is his ticket to anywhere?

But most of all, he wonders why. Why do the miners' kids lie in wait for the merchants' kids to rough them up on the way to and from school? Why do they call them *Zydek* and spit and jeer? Why, when the merchants are better off, better dressed, sometimes better educated and better mannered, do they seem to be a second class in Ashlymine? Because there aren't enough of them—that's why. That's how Hershy answers his own question.

"Prejudice," his father has told him. "Ignorance and prejudice. There's always one bunch that wants to blame another bunch for their troubles."

But why? Why do they have to stay in bunches? Why can't he be friends with a Polish kid like . . . like Lorsh Jabieski if he wants to? Sometimes Hershy looks at himself in the mirror and imagines himself as brawny instead of lean and wiry, blue eyed instead of brown, and flaxen haired instead of dark. Could he be a Pole, then? That isn't all there is to it, is it? Look at Morty Wise. He's blond and blue eyed and they rough him up just as much as Hershy. Whatever the magic quality is, Hershy would like to have it and be accepted by the rulers of Ashlymine as a regular person, not someone apart.

But if he doesn't want to be someone apart, why does he do his crab walk or sometimes zigzag up the hill, betting no one else in the world is doing just that thing that moment? Why does he hold his breath for the count of sixty? And why does he pore over the newspapers reading all about other people's lives, seeing if there is anyone like him anywhere. Well, there isn't. He is unique, an oddity among oddities, and he keeps making himself even more so, walking zigzag and crabwise. But at the same time, he wants very much to be part of *something*, something acceptable.

Quite by accident, he finds out what Alice Jabieski does in the afternoons. He goes home with Lenny to trade for baseball cards, and there is Alice helping Mrs. Gorin with the housework. She is pushing the carpet sweeper back and forth over the Axminister runner in the hall over the drugstore. Hershy is surprised and nearly speechless at first. He hasn't seen her since summer and she is taller, more muscular, more womanly, and less like a girl than a . . . a real person. She shines like Lorsh does and her teeth blaze as she cracks her gum. When she actually speaks to him, he realizes he's been staring.

"Whatcha lookin' at?" she asks, not stopping her sweeping.

Hershy, waiting for Lenny to return with his cards, searches his head for a reason and his throat for his voice.

"I didn't know I was." His voice starts out low and ends up high. He blushes.

"You goin' to the parade?" she asks.

It's a real conversation! A real conversation between himself and this special person! "Oh, sure, sure!" He knows she is speaking of the Decoration Day parade next week. It will go right by the store windows and he won't need to "go" to it at all.

"My pa marches. Does your pa?" Alice asks.

"No," Hershy says. "He doesn't. My pop doesn't march." How was this happening, this conversation here in Lenny's house, when she or her brother or any of them wouldn't even say a civil word to him in school or on the street?

"Wasn't he in the war?" Alice stops her sweeping.

"No."

"Why not?"

"His eyes. He has bad eyes."

"Oh, that's too bad. I'm carryin' a flag," Alice says.

"I'll watch ya."

She smiles at him, tilting her head over her arm sort of like a movie star. Mrs. Gorin appears in the doorway and Alice resumes her sweeping.

Lenny comes in and gives Hershy a poke. "Let's trade."

"Does she come here much?" Hershy asks when they are squatting on the Gorins' backstairs.

"Who?"

"Her. Alice."

"I dunno. Maybe twice a week. Why?"

"No reason," Hershy says. Lenny looks at him sharply.

"Hershy Marks has a crush on Alice Jabieski," Lenny announces in a singsong voice next day when they are all lying around the West Hill.

"I do not!" Hershy cries. "I don't have a crush on anyone. I don't even hardly know her."

"Ya like her," Lenny says. "Ya think I don't know? Maybe you're in love with her."

Hershy is furious. "How could I be in love with her?" he shouts. "She's a Polack, isn't she? How could I be in love with a Polish person?"

The logic of this puts an end to the taunting. Everyone knows how things are. But Hershy has no sooner said the words than the idea begins to bother him. How is it that all the same kind of people in Ashlymine seem to marry the same kind of people? Like the Polish are all married to Polish people and the Jewish people are all married to other Jewish people. And the few others—maybe a sprinkling of Irish and Germans—are probably all married to the same kind of people, as far as Hershy knows. How come? Is this like, say, squirrels stay with squirrels and cats stay with cats? Like that?

"No," Mr. Marks says, when Hershy hesitantly asks him about it that afternoon while they are sorting nuts and bolts in the store. "No, it's not like that. Animals are . . . well . . . made differently. They're different breeds."

"But maybe we're different breeds from the Poles," Hershy says.

"No. We're all the same. It's just, I suppose . . ." he hesitates. "I suppose we choose our own kind to sort of protect ourselves."

"Ya mean we don't *have* to?"

"Have to! Have to!" Mr. Marks is getting impatient.

"Could a person . . . a person like . . . like Morty, say, marry a person like . . . like . . . Alice Jabieski, if he wanted to?"

"Why? Why should he do that?" Mr. Marks asks. "What's the matter with the Greenberg girls, for instance? What's the matter with the Klein girls? You see! Even though this is a small town, there are plenty of nice girls."

"Yes, but what's the matter with Alice Jabieski?"

"Don't talk silly!"

"Is there a *reason?*" Hershy is getting upset. He hates to rile his father, but the damage is already done.

"Reason! Reason! Of course there's a reason. A Jewish boy is not supposed to marry a Polish girl. That's the reason. So don't be such a *nudzh.*"

"But who says so?" Hershy insists.

Mr. Marks becomes very quiet. "I don't know," he says. "It's just the way things are."

"The way things are! The way things are!" shouts Hershy.

"Don't yell," says Mr. Marks sharply. "What are you yelling about?"

"I dunno," Hershy says. "I dunno."

He goes down to the square and runs five laps. He doesn't have a watch but it feels like good time. His dream is to be a member of the high school team that goes down to the Penn Relays that are run every year in Philadelphia. He can imagine the team with Lorsh Jabieski, Tom Grabowski, maybe Georgie, and him, Hershy Marks. He knows he is going to be such a good runner that they are going to want him on the team. He feels this is a good dream, a reasonable hope. Of course, besides that, he would like to be a star, too. A sportswriter in the *Wilkes-Barre Record* said that one day someone would run a four-minute mile. What would happen if he could do that? Even the Poles would admire him, wouldn't they?

V

a musician in the family

"Huckleberries! huckle-berries!"

Hershy lies in bed on the sleeping porch listening to the huckster in the alley on a summer morning. He likes to stay in bed a little while and think. He imagines stuff. That sometime the postman will be there with the news that will change his life. He has no idea what it could be—an inheritance, a prize for being the best runner in Pennsylvania, some anonymous person paying off his father's mortgage debts, an offer of a job when he finishes school as . . . as a . . . a. . . .

"Huckleberries! Huck-le-beeeeeries!"

Mrs. Marks hurries onto the sleeping porch.

"Run down quick and get me ten cents worth of huckleberries, please."

"Huckleberries!" The cry rises on the warm air like a bird and circles over Hershy's head.

"Get up and throw something on," Mrs. Marks orders. Throw something on. Hershy has always liked the expression. Even hearing the hurry in his mother's voice, he irritates her by tossing his shirt in the air and catching it on his head. When she frowns, he says, "Ya said throw somethin' on, didn't ya?"

"Hershy!" She shakes him. "I want to make a pie."

"A pie!" That is a reason to hurry. Hershy pulls on his trousers, grabs a bowl from the kitchen, and sprints down the outside backstairs two at a time and across the dirt yard to the alley. A Polish kid he has never seen before is slowly pulling a little homemade wagon on which rocks a big bucket. The kid is skinny and dirty, but Hershy notices that he has a nice smile and sharp blue eyes.

"Hi!" Hershy says.

The kid ducks his head and says "Hi."

"Gimme a dipper, please."

He watches the boy put the cracked enamel dipper into the bucket and carefully measure a pint of midnight blue huckleberries, dusky with dew, into the bowl.

"Ya live around here?" Hershy asks.

"No, out near Coalville."

"Then, where d'ya go to school?"

Hershy doesn't know why he is so interested in what other people do, what their homes are like, but he is. He has walked through Coalville many times on the way to the Knob. Which of the unpainted, nearly black, wooden company houses does this boy live in? Coalville is right near the number three Atlas Colliery, its great black breaker standing high against the sky. The coal comes up from the mines and is sorted through a contraption of screens and chutes in the breaker. That is, when the mines are working. Right now, it is standing idle.

"Where d'ya go to school?" Hershy asks the kid again.

"Don't go."

"Don't go at all!" A lot of the older boys don't go because they work in the mines when they can. But a kid this age goes to school, Hershy knows that.

"No, but my brother goes. Me and my sister maybe are going to go next year . . . if the mines are working."

"What's the mines got to do with it?"

The boy shrugs. "I dunno. It just does."

Hershy pops a huckleberry into his mouth and holds it between his front teeth, slowly piercing the skin and letting the inky juice run onto his tongue. A perfect way to break his fast of the night. It occurs to him that you could talk to a Polish kid if you buy something from him, and he will talk back, too. So, if the Poles were the storekeepers and the Jews were

the miners, would things be different? How come
nobody ever thought of that? On the other hand,
Hershy knows he wouldn't want to earn his living
that way—walking through the cold black un-
derground passageways, doubled over in the low wet
tunnels, maybe for a mile, before you got to the vein
you were to mine. Digging through rock for no pay,
being paid maybe thirty cents a ton, and mining ten
tons on a good day. Working maybe two or three
days a week. Being in danger of cave-ins, gas explo-
sions, black lung.

"Where d'ya pick the berries?"

The boy looks up, suspicious. Is Hershy trying to
horn into his territory? He waves vaguely to the east.

"Ya must make a lot in a day," Hershy says, es-
timating the contents of the bucket.

"Not much with five kids in the family."

"Ya mean ya don't get to keep the money?"
Hershy asks.

"How else we goin' to eat?"

Hershy considers this. "Gee," he says. "Gee." He,
himself, uses the money he gets for delivering circu-
lars for the dress shop to buy gum, go to the movies,
buy pencils. Pencils are a particular interest. He likes
the brown penny ones. He likes to have a whole
bunch of them, all sharp, so that when anyone in
class is in need of a pencil—even a Polish kid—he
can lend him one.

The kid goes on his way down the alley where a
hobo is picking through Klein's garbage pail. Hershy

climbs the backstairs backwards. He figures there is probably nobody, in the Valley at least, who is doing that right this minute. Then he changes to every other step, backwards one step and frontwards the next. He figures no one else in the world is doing that right now. He tries to get a picture of that in his mind—the world as he knows it in the form of a globe in the classroom, and Ashlymine as a little spot that does not even appear on the globe, but is there anyhow. He has the globe in his mind, spinning through the universe, and he, Hershy Marks, doing this unique thing this minute with a bowl of huckle-berries in his hands.

"What's the mine got to do with whether this kid goes to school or not?" Hershy asks his father at the breakfast table, while his mother sprinkles snowy sugar over blue-black berries, getting some over Max's pudgy fingers, which are picking them out one by one.

"Just because you've got shoes, don't think everyone else has," Mr. Marks says.

"What happens to all those clothes everyone contributes in the big barrel in the town hall?"

"Who knows!" says Mr. Marks. "Even good intentions aren't perfect."

"I'll tell you why," says Mrs. Marks. "Some of those people take stuff relief gives them and they sell it for a few cents and then they buy bootleg whiskey." She looks angry. "The bums! And now the politicians are even talking about making liquor legal!" She throws up her hands.

"If he comes back," Hershy says, "I'm gonna give him my old black shoes. They're too tight."

"Don't you dare," Mrs. Marks says. "You can wear them if you have to, and after that I'll save them for Max. How do we know how long this Depression is going to last? We give plenty of things to the relief barrels. Maybe if Roosevelt is elected and he does the things he says, things will get better. But don't give anything away without asking."

"Maybe I could sell huckleberries," Hershy says.

"Things haven't gotten that bad, yet," Mr. Marks says.

Hershy doesn't think it sounds like such a bad thing—walking through the early morning field, wet with dew, picking huckleberries to help his family. A lot of older kids from miners' families work—the boys in the mines, the girls helping in stores or in houses like the Gorins'. When things were prosperous for the Marks family, they also had a Polish girl helping around the house, washing windows, cleaning the stove. Picking huckleberries couldn't be so bad.

"Get ready for your lesson," Mrs. Marks says. "Did you practice yesterday?"

Saturday morning has become an ordeal for Hershy since spring, but he doesn't know what to do about it. Mrs. Marks has set her heart on his learning to play the piano and she manages to save fifty cents a week from her food money to send him to Mr. Zosky for lessons.

"There's always been a musician in this family," says Mrs. Marks. "My brother Sam played the violin like a regular gypsy." The rickety upright piano came into the house years before as a hand-me-down from Mrs. Marks's older sister Milly, in Phillipsburg, New Jersey, who had been going to give it to the Salvation Army. But nobody in the Marks family could play and it had been standing silent under a rose-flowered scarf until Hershy was selected to carry on the family tradition.

Thus, all Saturday morning is spent getting to and from and being with Mr. Zosky. Even though he is Polish, he is the only music teacher in Ashlymine. Mr. Zosky teaches not only piano but also violin, trumpet, clarinet, accordion, and the ukulele. Hershy thinks maybe he would prefer the ukulele, but Mrs. Marks is dead set on the piano.

A visit to Mr. Zosky's house is like a trip to a vault. The air in it must have been trapped ever since Mr. Zosky moved in years ago and closed the doors and windows. The smells nauseate Hershy— cigar smoke, cat, garlic, cabbage, boiled clothes. Besides that, the inhaled air smells oily because Mr. Zosky—when he is not teaching piano, violin, trumpet, clarinet, accordion, or ukulele—is brewing furniture polish which he bottles and sells. What is in it is a mystery that Hershy has his own ideas about. Mrs.

Marks says it isn't very good, but she buys it to stay on Mr. Zosky's good side.

Like many of the houses in Ashlymine, Mr. Zosky's house has been badly affected by the settling of the mine beneath. The entire house leans alarmingly and the floor is separated from the wall by several inches. But this is not unusual. Hershy has been in many houses and stores with the same trouble. His father explained it to him long ago.

"They're supposed to leave pillars of coal to support the ground when they dig the coal out," Mr. Marks said. "Just like holding up the roof of a house. But when the vein of coal runs out, they rob the pillars. That means they start to take coal from the pillars and that's why there are these cave-ins and the big holes in the streets. We've been lucky, so far."

To his credit, Mr. Zosky has tried with much sweating, panting, and sighing to make a pianist out of Hershy Marks, but so far he has made little progress. He leans over Hershy like a great grunting shadow in his black rumpled suit, bending and unbending Hershy's fingers, putting them onto the right keys and moving them as if they were puppets.

"You're such a smart boy," Mr. Zosky moans in despair. "How come you're so stupid in this thing? Can't you *hear? You're hitting the wrong note!*" Then he excuses himself with a mutter and comes back a few minutes later, a new smell having been added to the bouquet—some cough medicine he seems to need frequently. Hershy has not heard him cough much, but Mr. Zosky always needs cough medicine during the lesson.

"I'm sorry, Mr. Zosky," Hershy says. "All the notes sound alike to me."

"Tone-deaf!" Mr. Zosky mourns and turns his eyes to the ceiling. "They send me even the tone-deaf to teach! Well, Zosky did not choose the path of teaching backward children, but Zosky will teach backward children, if that is what the Lord wants."

Hershy wonders if the Lord who directs Mr. Zosky to teach him is the regular God that they have in common, or is it Jesus Christ. Hershy thinks it would be interesting if it were Jesus Christ who was urging Mr. Zosky to make a pianist out of him. He wonders, in that case, if Jesus Christ might be punishing him for the sins the Poles believe him guilty of. On the other hand, Mr. Zosky seems to be suffering an awful lot, too, from the arrangement.

Years ago Mr. Zosky was supposed to have been an accompanist to a singer in New York, Mrs. Marks has told Hershy, but his mother became sick and he came home to care for her. He never got a chance to go away again, never married. "He's disappointed in life," Mrs. Marks said.

Disappointed in life! It is an interesting but scary idea. Hershy often worries about someone being disappointed in him—his mother about his music lessons, for instance—but he has not thought about being disappointed, himself, in what life may hold

for him. Another worry! He wonders if that huckleberry kid is disappointed in life already.

"That's A," yells Mr. Zosky, dashing from the
room again shouting, "A, A, A, not G! There's a
world of difference. One step and a world of difference." He yells from the back room. He returns
calmer. "Try again."

Hershy thinks he might have to throw up from
the smells. But if he does, what will he throw up
into? He selects a big decorated china bowl near the
door where Mr. Zosky throws his cigar butts.

Though Mr. Zosky is exasperated with Hershy,
thinks him a hopeless case, and says so, he isn't really
nasty. Even when he is upset, he does not call him
Zydek. But Hershy wonders if he *thinks* it. Does Mr.
Zosky secretly despise him?

"Does your mother need any more furniture
polish?" Mr. Zosky asks when the lesson is over and
he has collapsed, fanning himself, in a chair with
springs that hang to the floor.

"I'll ask her," says Hershy, opening the door and
escaping into the air.

He walks back from Mr. Zosky's in a zigzag
course. It is something he might do anyway, to make
him unique, but it has a practical side—it makes it
possible to avoid groups of approaching Polish kids.
He is in enemy country. It makes the trip longer, but
on the way he examines his discontentment. In the

first place he is wasting every Saturday morning when he could be playing ball or just hanging around with the kids. Today, for instance, Sheldon and Morty have probably already left for a hike up Newbury Knob. Hershy hates to miss hikes up to the Knob. It is wilderness. There are snakes and foxes, and some people claim there are still bears there. What Hershy likes best about the high view is that the sky goes not only up but down.

The second reason Hershy is discontented is that he keeps feeling like a failure. It is a feeling that makes him miserable. He does well in school and well enough in *cheder,* but at piano he is a disaster. If sticking to it were the answer, he is doing that and it isn't working.

In the third place, is it right to waste the money? He knows the store is in bad shape, business is rotten. And in the fourth place, he feels guilty having music lessons while some kids, like that kid this morning, are out selling huckleberries to help their families. He tries to explain this to Mrs. Marks.

"Don't talk nonsense," she says. "How is it going to help that kid if you don't take piano lessons?"

"But what about the starving children ya always talk about?"

"Don't be fresh," Mrs. Marks snaps.

"I'm not. I mean it." You can't explain things to anyone.

Even his practicing at the old upright in the sitting room does not persuade his mother that he is no musician. She listens to him laboring over the exercises and his first "piece" and nods and smiles.

He thinks maybe she is tone-deaf, too.

"So, now, play something," says Mr. Marks as he comes into the sitting room that evening. "All summer I hear scales down in the store, but I don't hear any tunes. So now, let's hear you play something."

"Ah, Pop!"

"Come on, Hershy, show your father how you can play," Mrs. Marks urges.

"Play, Hersh!" yells Max.

"I can't play."

"He can't play, he says," Mrs. Marks says. "All spring and summer he's been taking lessons."

"Mom, ya don't understand. I'm tone-deaf." He hates to say it. To see her disappointment.

But she is only angry. "You've got a hundred percent perfect hearing so don't give excuses. Play."

Hershy sits down at the piano and runs the C scale.

"Go on," says Mr. Marks. "Play a tune. The scale I heard already." He looks accusingly at Mrs. Marks.

Hershy looks miserably at them and then he gets up and bolts from the room. He does not know how he can stand this new burden he is putting upon them—the failed musician.

"Take Max with you this morning," Mrs. Marks says the next Saturday.

"But Mom, I wanna meet the kids after my lesson," Hershy complains.

"So, take Max with you to meet the kids. It's not such a terrible thing to ask you to take your little brother with you on a Saturday morning when I have to go out."

Max doesn't walk fast enough, that's one trouble. His short legs have to take two strides to each of Hershy's.

"Wait for me, Hersh," Max pants.

"Ya wanted to come along so ya gotta keep up."

"I didn't wanna. She made me."

So! Max is put upon, too.

While they wait for Mr. Zosky to come from the back room, Hershy sits on the greasy velvet sofa and Max pokes at the piano.

"It smells in here," Max complains. Then he starts to hum and pick out a tune by trial and error. "My country 'tis . . . 'tis . . . 'tis . . . of thee . . ."

Even Max can pick out a tune, Hershy mourns. Isn't there some point when Mr. Zosky will just throw him out in desperation? He thinks not. Mr. Zosky is not likely to do that because he will lose his fifty cents a week, plus the occasional sale of furniture polish.

It embarrasses Hershy to be in Mr. Zosky's house, the house of a Pole. He is embarrassed by his fascination with the holy pictures, gold and red, the mother and child with halos, a gold cross hanging over the piano. He feels not only an outsider to music but a stranger in this strange-smelling, foreign house. Does Mr. Zosky regard him as an intruder? Does he tolerate Hershy only because he needs the money from the lessons? Like his father is polite to the Poles in the store because he needs their business? But, then, Mr. Zosky sometimes gives Hershy a good postage stamp from mail he gets from an aunt in Poland because he knows Hershy saves them.

Max plays on. "Land of . . . of . . . the pilgrims' . . ."

From the back, Mr. Zosky calls, "Well, *that's* something like it! When did you get the wax out of your ears?" And then he appears in the doorway, wiping the cough syrup from his lips. He sees Max, and moans, "I knew it was too good to be true. Who's this?"

"This is my kid brother, Max."

"You like the piano, Max?" Mr. Zosky asks.

"It's okay," Max says.

"Now, *him*," Mr. Zosky says, "I could teach. How come they sent me you?" Hershy wonders how many ways Mr. Zosky can find to insult him.

"That," continues Mr. Zosky, as Max goes on picking out the tune, "is the musician in the family. He's got, at least, an ear."

Desperation and inspiration hit Hershy at once. "Mr. Zosky," he says, "why don't ya give Max a lesson today?"

The dim bulb in Mr. Zosky's face lights and then goes out. "What would your mother say?"

"She won't care." His heart misses a beat at this statement which, deep inside, he isn't so sure about. "All she wants is one musician in the family and you say Max is it." He is convincing himself and Mr. Zosky at the same time. "Just show him how to play something. *Anything!*" Hershy is begging. He is begging a Pole.

Mr. Zosky hesitates a second, but only a second. The temptation to deal with a hearing ear is too great to resist. He spends an hour showing Max how to hold his hands on the keys and how to play "America" from start to finish in the treble clef. He does not leave the piano even once to take his cough medicine.

After supper, Hershy grabs Max by the arm and drags him into the sitting room.

"Play the tune," he hisses, helping him up onto the piano stool. "Play loud."

"I don't want to," Max says.

"Play it!" Hershy growls ominously.

Sticking out his lower lip and putting his pudgy hands on the piano, Max begins to play his piece and soon becomes caught up in humming and playing.

Mr. Marks appears in the doorway. "At last! A tune!" he exclaims. And then he sees Max. "Fanny, look at this!"

Mrs. Marks is speechless at first, then she swoops

down on the piano and envelops Max in her arms.
"My little baby," she cries. "He plays the piano! And
without a lesson in his life!" She turns and glares at
Hershy. "Look! Look what your little baby brother
can do."

"He's a genius," says Hershy. "A real musician.
Why don't ya give him lessons with Mr. Zosky?"

"Lessons for two we can't manage right now,"
Mrs. Marks says regretfully.

"Give him mine," Hershy says. "Give him mine."

Mrs. Marks looks at him closely. "You wouldn't
mind?" she asks. "You wouldn't mind if your little
brother has lessons and you don't?"

"Nah," Hershy says. "I had some lessons already."

"You're a good boy," says Mrs. Marks. "A real
brother. Play some more, Max."

"No," Max says, "not now."

"All right, later," Mrs. Marks says. "You'll play it
later?"

"Yes," Max says. "I'll play around nine o'clock."

"You go to bed at nine o'clock," Mrs. Marks says.

"Not anymore," says Max.

VI

the eclipse

THE CHICKENS under Hershy's and Sheldon's arms are struggling in their newspapers on the way to the ritual slaughter. One of Hershy's bad dreams is the chicken gaining its freedom and taking off down the street. It has happened once with Hershy whirling around after it, half-crazy with the idea of what would happen to him if the dinner flew away. To make it worse there were witnesses to his humiliation. Jeers and cheers arose around him:

"Go it, chicken!"

"Where's that chicken taking that kid?"

"That chicken don't want to be et by *Zydeks*."

"Which one is the chicken?"

Was Lorsh Jabieski one of the spectators? Hershy

wasn't sure. He thought he might have seen him out of the corner of his eye. Just the thought of it made him feel worse. He finally threw himself full length on the chicken, nearly smothering himself in feathers, and carried the flapping and squawking bird by the feet the rest of the way.

Now the chicken's wriggling makes him nervous, but he holds on firmly with two hands while Sheldon imparts information. One thing about Sheldon, he remembers stuff. Ask Sheldon how far from Ashlymine to Harrisburg and he can tell you. Ask him how far from Ashlymine to the moon and he can tell you that, too.

"The reason there's gonna be a total eclipse of the sun," says Sheldon, "is because the moon is gonna be between the sun and the earth. Can't ya get that straight? Even though the moon is a lot smaller than the sun, it's a lot nearer, see. So it seems bigger. Get it? Like, hold your thumb right up in front of your face."

"I can't," Hershy says. "I don't wanna drop this chicken."

"Go ahead, I'll help ya hold the chicken with one hand." Hershy holds up his thumb. "Okay, now turn around so you're looking at that rock over there. Okay. Can ya see the rock?"

"Yeah."

"Now move your finger till ya can't see the rock."

Hershy moves his thumb until it blocks out the rock.

"Well then," Sheldon says. "Your finger is smaller than the rock but it can hide it. Right? That's the way it is with the moon and the sun. Now do ya get it?"

"Yeah!" Hershy says.

"So, anyhow," Sheldon goes on, "ya can't look into the sun because ya could go blind. So ya have to watch the eclipse through something."

"Like what?"

"Like a piece of real black exposed negative from a camera. Or else smoked glass. I don't have film but I'm gonna try and get a piece of glass and smoke it up with a candle."

"We got glass in the store," Hershy says. "Lots of glass. Probably my father will cut a couple of pieces for us."

"Great," Sheldon says.

While Rabbi Aaron slaughters the chicken at the back door of the *shul,* Hershy looks up at the clouds. He prefers not to watch. Something about the way the rabbi does this and the prayers he thinks when he does it makes the chicken proper for a Jewish table.

"So, can I come over after supper and we'll fix up some glass for the eclipse?" Sheldon asks as they walk back to Market Street.

"Okay," Hershy says, the chicken now limp in the newspapers under his arm. It is easier to carry, but somehow he likes it even less.

At home, Hershy turns his eyes away from the sink where the chicken, which recently kicked beneath his arm, lies disjointed under a layer of coarse salt, while his mother boils water with which to scald and clean it. Kosher meat means fresh clean meat, but this so recently alive chicken does not tempt Hershy's appetite. He looks instead at the newspaper spread on the kitchen table. This summer, one of the hardware salesmen from New York has been leaving his *New York Times* for Mr. Marks. Hershy has found out that this newspaper tells a lot more about the world than the *Ashlymine News* or even the *Wilkes-Barre Record*. For months there has been more and more trouble in Germany. A couple of weeks ago President Hindenburg even offered Hitler a place in the government, but Hitler said no, what he wanted was to have the powers of a dictator, like Mussolini in Italy. The *Times* says that what happens in Germany now "depends on the whim of Hitler and a group of fanatics who surround him."

"Eat!" Mrs. Marks says as the soup steams in front of Hershy. But he keeps seeing the soup transformed into the chicken struggling beneath his arm and into the blood and feathers on the bare ground behind the *shul*.

"Not hungry," he says, reaching for the big golden braided *challah*.

Mrs. Marks rolls her eyes towards the ceiling and

addresses it. "Not hungry for good hot soup, but he stuffs himself with bread!"

"Pop?"

"What's on your mind?"

"Nothin'. I just wondered if I could have a couple of pieces of glass from the store."

"Glass? I'm sort of going out of the glass business."

"I only need a couple of tiny pieces. I wanna smoke 'em to watch the eclipse."

"Oh, sure. I've got plenty for that."

"How come you're going out of the glass business?" Mrs. Marks asks.

"I'm just not reordering," Mr. Marks says, waving away the question. "Listen, there are a lot of things I'm not reordering. The suppliers want cash on delivery now. I'm short."

"I told you not to order so many tools from Levin when he came around last month. It took too much money. What do you need such a large stock of tools for? Who's going to buy them?"

"Listen, Levin has troubles, too. He sells good tools, beautiful Stanley tools." Mr. Marks blows on his soup.

"That's no reason you should buy them if you don't have customers to buy and pay."

"The mines have to work sometime. People will have to have tools. The mines are bound to work soon. The country has to have coal."

"Who says so? Did you ever hear of oil?" Mrs.

Marks is upset and talking, but she has finished her soup.

"Oh Fanny, for heaven's sake! They'll always use coal."

"Eat!" says Mrs. Marks.

Two hawkers are standing in the square selling darkened film and smoked glass.

"Why didn't we think of that?" mourns Sheldon. "We could've made a fortune."

"Here y'are! See the eclipse. A dime. Ten cents." They shout. People are buying, too. One hawker has fastened the film to cardboard and cut out a place for the nose. He calls them Eclipse-o-Scopes. They are selling for a quarter.

"We coulda done that," Sheldon repeats. He is upset by his failure to see the business opportunity.

"We can do it next year," says Morty, who has joined them.

"Next year! You dope!" Sheldon says. "It'll be hundreds of years before there's another total eclipse around here."

Even Hershy can't imagine that. Hundreds of years until this identical thing happens again in Ashlymine.

Now the bright summer day seems to cloud over. You might think a storm is coming or that it is later in the day than you think. People walking along the street hurry to finish their business before the eclipse, as if this is the last chance.

Hershy, Sheldon, and Morty sit at the foot of the Pulaski statue and just wait. As it grows darker, the merchants and their families emerge from the stores. More people gather, staring at the changing sun through film or glass. The square looks like a big masquerade. Hershy finds himself whispering.

"How long does it last?"

"I dunno," whispers Sheldon.

The moon's shadow spreads slowly and then, it seems, more rapidly across the face of the sun. Just before the sun is completely covered, a great red light seems to surround the moon's dark shape. Then a sort of silvery ring spreads around the two heavenly bodies.

And then it is dark, very dark. The trolley which runs up Main Street has come to a full stop and the people in it crane their necks to view the eclipse. The hawkers run alongside selling Eclipse-o-Scopes. Time is suspended. Reality changes. In the strange and eerie darkness, Hershy feels a tap on the shoulder. He jumps.

"Lemme look through that, okay?"

Hershy turns quickly. It sounds like—it is! Lorsh Jabieski and Georgie are standing there, hands across eyes, peeking through fingers.

"Give us a loan of that. Okay?"

"Here!" Hershy thrusts the glass at Lorsh. "Take it, I have another." He reaches into his pocket and carefully removes and unwraps a jagged piece he had cut badly last night. He watches the eclipse but also looks sideways at Lorsh looking at the sun through *his,* Hershy's, glass!

There, in the strange dark, cast by a shadow out in space, in touch with the mysteries of the earth, in touch with the motion of moon and sun, in direct view of distant planets, they witness together through smoked glass the first total eclipse of the sun to be seen from that part of the world in hundreds of years.

How long does the sun hide completely? A minute and nine-tenths. Not nearly long enough, Hershy thinks. Then the moon very slowly moves from west to east across the face of the sun, and gradually the sun reemerges on the other side of the shadow. The day gradually brightens and the earth, which has been transformed for a time, returns to normal. People begin to talk and move again, just like Hershy has seen in the movies when the projectionist stops the film and then starts it again. Time resumes.

Lorsh hands Hershy the glass. "Thanks," he says, and turning sharply, leaves.

Hershy looks about. Nothing has changed. The day is the same as it was only a short while ago. There is nothing to show that anything spectacular has happened in this part of the world except smudged pieces of smoked glass.

VII

the new one

THE LOW afternoon sun touches the new rabbi's head to form a nearly perfect halo. Hershy Marks regards this phenomenon with wonder and fear. Wonder, because it seems to him that people sometimes look exactly like pictures in books and he wonders if they have come to look that way by looking at the pictures. But the rabbi couldn't really know that the sun was going to come through the classroom window just now, and at that angle. Or could he? Fear, because, at the beginning of the new fall term, it is not yet known if the new rabbi is a hitter. It was possible to perform all kinds of mischief around the old rabbi, whose sight had been failing, too, and whose step was slow.

This hour of Hebrew education, after a full day in school, is made more tolerable through pranks and antics. Next year all this will be over for some of them; each boy will have his *Bar Mitzvah* at the age of thirteen—he will become a man. Hershy has never understood how one day someone can be a boy and the next a man, but he knows it is so. Until then, study indoors when one could be outside playing ball, the odd geometry of the Hebrew letters, the guttural words, are all part of the boys' daily life.

Morty Wise is probably the cleverest cut-up in the class. He does imitations of everyone in town. Before the new rabbi is there two days, Morty has perfected an impersonation so good that he even appears to have gaunt high cheeks when, in fact, he is round faced.

Although Hershy can always break up the class with his fish face or his rubberman tricks, he has to admit Morty's act is much funnier. Morty can also imitate the motor of any car you can name—a Dodge, a Ford, an Essex. He does terrific gear changes, too. But his newest trick is an imitation of the new rabbi eating his supper, lifting fish bones daintily with his fork and knife, chewing with his prominent front teeth. That convulses everyone.

Rabbi Gold went to Wises' for supper the first night of his arrival and—as is the custom with the town's rabbi—has circulated among the families, having supper with one or another of them nearly every evening. What does the rabbi's wife do for

supper? Hershy wonders. When the old rabbi used
to come to the Marks house for supper, Hershy
wished to ask this question. But his wife was an old
woman, possibly without teeth. Perhaps all she could
eat was tea and mush. However, this new rabbi's wife
is something else again. A sort of round lady with
very blond soft hair, blue eyes, and nice white teeth.
Nothing at all like any rabbi's wife Hershy could
imagine.

The night the rabbi came to dine at his house,
Hershy fantasized as the conversation dragged on
around him. He thought he could take a slice of pot
roast and piece of potato pudding in a big paper
napkin and sneak it over to Mrs. Gold. Why not? Did
the rabbi want her to starve to death? Was he
ashamed of her? What kind of way was this to treat a
gorgeous person like her!

He was called back from his suppertime dream
by some change in the key of the conversation. The
rabbi was intoning his name.

"Herschel. Why eight lights?"

Hershy raised his eyebrows as if thinking. In fact,
he was waking himself up. He didn't hear a word
that preceded his name. But eight lights—what else
could it be?

"Because the oil lasted eight days in the lamp of
the temple when there really wasn't enough oil for
that."

The rabbi regarded him, unimpressed. "In *cheder*," he said, "I would strongly advise you against

daydreaming." So he *was* a hitter! Hershy blushed, but wasn't the man a guest at their table? Should he be threatening?

Now in *cheder,* Rabbi Gold has not, as yet, shown his colors. The ruler remains on the desk where it was left by the old rabbi. But class mischief has been suspended all week and a tense courtesy exists. There is suspense on both sides.

The class has been sitting stiffly and nervously as the rabbi tests its knowledge of Hebrew. Hershy wants to move his knees from under the desk, which is low and crowding his lengthening legs, but he fears to creak the seat and call attention to himself. It is good he will be having his *Bar Mitzvah* next year. His knees won't fit under the desk much longer.

Rabbi Gold is holding a prayer book open to the psalms. He pushes the book in front of Morty Wise and holds one of his hands over the English translation.

"Read and translate," Rabbi Gold says.

Morty starts to read. *"Yhishem adonai m'ro-roch me-at-to v'ad-o-lom."*

Morty keeps his finger on the last word he has read and raises his head, mouth open.

"Translate. Begin," Rabbi Gold says.

"Ya mean . . ."

"I mean translate the sentence you have just read into English."

"Can't," Morty mutters.

"What did you say?"

"Can't. Dunno what it means."

"You-don't-know-what-it-means!" Rabbi Gold says, as if he is teaching each of the words to a foreigner who is also deaf and dumb. His tone strikes a match to the tension which fills the room like helium. There is a loud crack. Has a ruler come down on Morty's dull head? No. It is just the rabbi cracking his knuckles in what Hershy has to admit is a unique and arresting manner. How does he do that?

"Next!" snaps the rabbi, stepping up to Lenny Gorin. "Read." He points.

"Mimmizrah she-mesh ad m'vo-o . . . m'hul-lol shem adonai."

"Translate."

"Can't," Lenny says, sliding to the other side of his chair and not even trying.

There go the rabbi's knuckles. Crack! It is a judgment. Harsh. It must hurt! Hershy wants to yell to Rabbi Gold not to do that. Now he risks moving his knees from under the desk. Only part of him is really distressed, even though the rabbi is approaching. The inquisition cannot be as bad as the suspense of this last week.

"All right," Rabbi Gold says, pushing the book at Hershy. "Is there *anything* on this page you can read and translate?"

"Halelu is praise," Hershy scans the page.

The rabbi glares at him. "A genius! Go on."

"Adonai is God."

"Go on."

"I think that's all I know."

"That's all you know. How long have you been studying Hebrew?"

"Maybe four years."

"And you know two words."

"I know a lot of words. I just don't know what they all mean."

"Then what good are they?"

Hershy considers this. "We can say the prayers."

"Yes, but you don't know what you're saying."

Is the rabbi going to crack his knuckles? If he is, Hershy wishes he would do it and get it over with. Waiting for the rabbi's self-inflicted pain is too painful. But the crack does not come. Instead Rabbi Gold stands silent, then he picks up the book and reads in a great deep voice.

"Who is like unto the Lord our God
   That is enthroned on high
   That looketh down low
   Upon heaven and upon earth?
   Who raiseth up the needy out of the dunghill;
   That he may set him with princes
   Even with the princes of His people.
   Who maketh the barren woman to dwell in her house
   As a joyful mother of children.
   Hallelujah."

First there is silence. Then the rabbi says, "Those, my young friends, are the same words sung in ancient days and which are still read and sung today, thousands of years later, in many languages, by Jew and Christian. To read, to study, to understand is why you are here, not . . ." his voice rises, "not to recite words like some . . . some parrots in pants and sneakers." The class breaks into nervous and relieved laughter.

Behind Rabbi Gold's back—now that the tension has broken—Morty is doing his imitation of the rabbi, sucking in his cheeks, raising his brows, pinching his nose, and sticking out his teeth. Hershy looks down at his book so as not to laugh. The rabbi starts to turn and Morty's face immediately blows up like the balloon it more closely resembles normally. Now Rabbi Gold walks to the front of the room and sits in a chair. He puts his head in his hands for a few seconds and then he looks up.

"Children," he says. "Boys. Young men. Why are we here?" He answers himself. "We are here so that I may help you to learn the ancient laws, the ancient ways, of your ancestors. We are here to prepare you to carry on great Judaic traditions, so that next year you may join the congregation and participate in the life of an imperishable people who have survived to worship in their own way despite persecutions and prejudice throughout the ages. Continuity, continuance, perpetuation. Remember the ways of your fathers as your children will remember you." He pauses to see the variety of reactions to his words. He smiles. "Maybe you would rather think you are the members of a relay team, passing the baton. You are. Don't drop it."

Hershy wonders if the rabbi is speaking directly to him. Does he guess his deepest dreams of glory?

"Well, those are some of the reasons you are here—not to waste a precious hour every day when you might like to play ball."

Hershy's eyes widen. He knows, all right!

"Not to learn by rote a few words that you do not understand. If you do not understand, ask. We will learn together, not only the Hebrew language but thought, ideas. In ancient days the Hebrew children were taught a love of learning by being given honey cakes in the shape of letters when they went to school. Today we do not coax you."

Hershy raises his hand and then puts it down again, fast.

"Yes? You have a question?"

"No," he says. "I forgot it."

He has a question, all right, but he doesn't dare ask it. Why can't everyone have the same religion? What's so great about one religion that makes it better than any other? They all believe in God, don't they? Look, they use a lot of the same prayers, don't they? Like the psalm the rabbi just read. It seems so simple and so obvious that Hershy can't understand why everyone else can't see it. But—like changing the name of their baseball team—if it were such a good idea, surely someone else would think of it, wouldn't they?

Hershy shoots his hand up again. It is now or never. "I got another question."

"Go ahead," the rabbi says.

"I want to ask ya about—about Jesus Christ." Hershy flushes because the name is strange on his tongue. Morty claps his hand over his head. Rabbi Gold looks surprised.

"What do you want to know?" he asks. Hershy thinks he probably won't get an answer but charges ahead, anyway.

"Did we really kill Christ like the kids say?"

"What kids?"

"The Polacks."

Rabbi Gold sits quietly for a minute. Hershy just hopes the rabbi won't give him a hit like Morty said the old rabbi did, and even more than that, he hopes the new rabbi won't crack his own knuckles in that agonizing way.

"First," Rabbi Gold says, "why do you call them Polacks?"

"That's what they are."

"And you are *Zydeks* to them."

"But—but—"

"But nothing. Pole, Polish boy, not Polack. In fact, just 'boy' would be best. Now, as to your question: From all the reading I have done, I'd say a lot of people had a hand in it. You must remember that nearly everyone was Jewish in Jerusalem, in those days, except for the Romans—even Jesus Christ, himself, and his disciples."

"But who did it?" Hershy asks. He isn't going to get an answer, is he?

"Well, according to the New Testament, Christ was betrayed by his own disciple, Judas. He was tried by the Sanhedrin, a Jewish court. A Roman, Pontius Pilate, sentenced him. Roman soldiers nailed him to the cross. Crucifixion was not a Jewish way of execution."

Hershy looks confused. "So, who really killed him?"

"Well, if we are to believe what has been written, I think we must say that humanity killed him—or inhumanity—as it has killed others and will kill still others."

"But then why do the Polish kids hate us?"

The rabbi shakes his head. "Years and years," he says. "Prejudice. If we could change it with a wish, it would be changed. Perhaps someday there will be enlightenment. Perhaps by being the best of what and who we are, by touching just one person who hates, people will learn. 'Thou shalt love thy neighbor as thyself.' We are taught that. Tolerance. Tell me," he addresses Hershy. "Do you hate—no 'hate' is too strong a word—do you dislike the Poles?"

Me? Hershy thinks. He admires, indeed longs to be, Lorsh Jabieski, and if he cannot be him, he would like to be one of his allies. He thinks Alice Jabieski is gorgeous and nice, too. Tom Grabowski is a pain in the neck and Georgie is terrifying. He doesn't dislike Mr. Zosky, but neither does he enjoy being with him because he smells and teaches the piano.

"I like some of them," he says, "and I don't like some of them."

Rabbi Gold smiles. "That," he says, "is probably just as it should be. Now, go play ball. But remember who you are—part of a long strong chain."

So! He *was* part of something big—not just the merchants of Ashlymine—but an important something. Astounding!

"Now get out of here," says Rabbi Gold.

VIII

the wager

SNOW, FOLLOWED by a cold snap, hits the town in early February. Fresh snow on the hills and the streets instantly transforms the town from drab gray to magnificent white. There are days of fast action: first, just tramping down the snow; then belly-whopping; and finally, when all is slick and icy, the most daring sport of all—sliding down the hill on one's feet.

The sliding begins just below the school and ends in the jog where Kosciusko Street becomes Market. Only the bravest or the most foolish even start the journey. The rest stand along the sides of the hill and watch, cheer, jeer, or take short slides starting just a few feet from the bottom.

95

Lorsh Jabieski is the champ, hands down. He takes a pose at the top of the hill, flexes his knees, squints down the hill to get a line on any bumps to be avoided, and then, leaning forward, he starts the descent, balancing forward and back, leaning, twisting, and finishing gloriously, arms outflung, on his feet the whole way, while the crowd cheers.

Hershy, brave but unbalanced, tries the last ten feet of the hill. He slides a few feet, churning wildly, then crashes onto the icy road, and ends up in the snowbank, laughing.

Lenny Gorin stands at the top of the hill daring one and all to do it and betting they can't. "Betcha a million dollars ya won't dare do it."

Nutty Cohen finally has enough of Lenny. "Do it yourself! Let's see ya!" he cries, waving his fat arms in Lenny's face.

"Yeah," Morty Wise puts in a dig. He is tired of Lenny's nagging, too. "Yeah, let's see ya risk yer own neck."

Lenny stares at them, surprised. People are used to his extravagant wagers. They don't usually dare him.

"What about it, Lenny?" Nutty asks in his slow voice, every word weighing a full pound.

"I'm gonna do it when I feel like it," says Lenny.

"Why don't you do it now, Lenny?" urges Sheldon. "We'd all like to see a real expert." He nudges Hershy. Hershy laughs.

"Okay, okay! You just watch me," says Lenny,

slowly shuffling up to the brink of the slide. He looks down the hill frowning, then back at his pals. They are all grinning and gesturing.

"Ah!" Lenny sighs, shaking his head. Then he leans forward to look down Kosciusko Street, flexes his knees as Lorsh did, bending and unbending, at which point Nutty runs up and gives the crucial shove that starts him down the hill. In a second Lenny is sliding on the seat of his pants, ice flying up around him as he tears down the hill, his arms grabbing first at air and then at the icy roadway.

Laughter crashes down the hill to where he piles up in the snowbank. At first he stays quite still, then, he slowly unfolds himself, stands up, and shakes the ice and snow from his clothes. The laughter becomes a roar—Lenny has torn a hole in his knickers. He cranes his neck to regard the damage. Fury and tears hit him at the same time and he turns and runs down Market Street, slipping, sliding, and falling, followed all the way by the sound of his schoolmates' howls.

Morty bangs his fist against his pants leg in a fit of delight. "Did ya see the look on his face?" he cries, between bursts of high-pitched laughter. "That should take care of his big mouth for a while!"

Lenny isn't in school the next day. His mother has sent a note, just like the notes she has written many times before, saying Lenny has run away again.

"Where does he run to, anyway?" Sheldon asks. "And in the cold?"

"He doesn't say," Hershy answers. "He never tells."

"Maybe he goes to Grabowski's farm and hides in the barn. He could get milk from the cow and eggs from the chickens and keep warm in the hay," Sheldon suggests.

"Maybe," Morty says, "but Grabowski might find him. How about the Knob? Maybe he is hiding in that cave up on the Knob."

"I don't think he would go there anymore after the last time," Hershy answers.

A cold Saturday afternoon late last fall was the last time they were all up on Newbury Knob. Everybody packed a peanut butter or salami sandwich and an orange or something and they hiked up the great hill that hangs over the town, its knobby summit looking like an enormous fist clenched to strike. They clambered up the steep trail, tramping on fallen leaves, panting, and straining. Then they threw themselves on the rocks, ate their lunches, and lolled around like Roman senators. Suddenly there was a cry from below.

"Help! Help me!" It sounded far away. Quickly they looked around the Knob. Lenny wasn't there. They threw themselves down on the edge, heads hanging over, looking in terror down into the ravine. Nothing could be seen in the great cavernous drop to the trees below.

"Help me! Help me!" came the voice, distant, fading.

"We gotta get help!" cried Hershy, and they ran down the mountain and all the way into town.

Lenny's mother and father closed the drugstore and rushed to the foot of the hill, Mrs. Gorin red eyed and Mr. Gorin tense and breathing rapidly. The police sent three men with ropes up the Knob.

They found Lenny in five minutes. He responded to their call from a small ledge directly under the fist of the Knob where the boys had been—a little shelf where he had climbed as a prank. He had been able to get down into it but he had not known he could not get out until after the other boys had run for help. Lenny was glad to see the policemen, but they bawled him out and he was frightened and sheepish. His mother whacked him right in front of everyone.

After the sliding incident Lenny stayed out of school two days and is given detention for a week after he returns.

"Where did ya go, Lenny?" Sheldon wants to know.

"Wouldn't ya like to know," is Lenny's reply.

The cold snap continues. The mines are working now to supply the country with much-needed fuel. The sharp mine whistle blows every morning and the deep chill of winter sends the miners' children onto the slag heaps to pick coal for the stoves.

On days like this, when the darkness falls early and Hershy approaches his home and the family store after *cheder* in winter, it is a nice feeling to see the store lit up. Every month, though, another store fails and goes out of business and there are fewer and fewer lights at night.

When he enters the store, the warm smells of rubber and metal and the oil that his father puts on the floor are welcoming and familiar. There are no customers, a fact that Hershy has noticed more and more often. His father, with a green eyeshade, is sitting on a stool with a book of accounts open in front of him. He looks up and gives Hershy a closed-mouth smile, nodding his head in welcome, but keeping his place in the book.

Hershy knows what his father is doing. He is trying to see which people who owe him money can be expected to pay him soon. And his father knows the answer. Hardly any. Why does he give so many people credit! And then, when the mines do start to work and the miners have a little money, do they come and pay their bills? They do not. They go over to Nanticoke or into Wilkes-Barre and buy what they need instead of showing their money in Ashlymine where they would be expected to pay a little on account. His father has explained this to Hershy before.

And this is why his father has this quiet anger about the miners—anger banked like the coal stove at night. Mr. Marks resents them as much as they resent owing him money. Hershy can't blame him. He has thought about it a lot and, as he walks upstairs with his father this evening, he thinks that maybe the real trouble isn't so much about Christ—not here in Ashlymine, though maybe it was in olden times in Jerusalem. The trouble here isn't even just the Poles not liking the Jews. It's the miners not liking the storekeepers, and the storekeepers not liking the miners.

"So why do ya keep giving them credit?" Hershy asks, as they go up to supper.

"You want me to go out of business!" his father replies. "I might have to do that anyhow. Besides, what should the poor fellows do—go into the mines without a lamp because I won't give them some carbide? Lose a day's work? Then, I surely wouldn't get paid!"

Hershy considers this. Maybe next month everything will get better because, in March, Mr. Roosevelt is going to be inaugurated as the new President and a lot of things could happen. That's what people say. But Hershy still thinks it is unfair for his father to be out the money and worried all the time.

"But why won't they pay when they have the money?" Hershy persists, even though he knows the answer.

"Because there's no way they can catch up. Because . . ."

"Because you're a *schnook*," offers Mrs. Marks. "Because your father would rather have us starve than those miners."

"Now you're starving?" Mr. Marks asks.

"You know what I mean." Mrs. Marks puts the cold stuffed veal on a plate and surrounds it with cold peas. She puts it next to the bowl of applesauce on the table. "Eat," she says.

After supper in winter they turn on the radio and listen to "Amos and Andy." Mr. Marks laughs a lot at Amos and Andy and Hershy likes to listen because he likes to see his father double up laughing. He sometimes listens to "Little Orphan Annie" when Max tunes it in before supper, but he pretends not to be listening. On a Saturday, he likes to tune in to the Paul Whiteman band. He may be no musician, but he really likes the snappy jazz rhythms. He taps his feet and drums on the table with a couple of spoons, with Kaiser howling and barking the whole time and his mother yelling, "Turn off that noise!"

In winter, Hershy manages to get to the library about twice a week, and he can read at least two books at once. Right now he is reading a Frank Merriwell book. Frank is a terrific fellow, plays the perfect game, and always comes through. For some reason, Hershy doubts that Frank is Jewish. He is also reading about Nick Carter, a great detective, and he has also started a book that the librarian suggested to him, *The Last of the Mohicans*, by James Fenimore

Cooper. And, of course, he keeps up with the news in the *Wilkes-Barre Record.* Just the other day Hitler finally got to be Chancellor in Germany. The cold winter evenings pass this way. It isn't as exciting as in spring when a person can get outside and throw a ball around after supper, but it's okay.

It continues cold, and Sunday afternoon Sheldon stops by to ask Hershy to come down to the river. Hershy grabs his lumber jacket and crams his cap onto his head.

"What's doin' at the river?" he asks as they walk down lower Market Street towards the railroad bridge. Kaiser lopes along behind them. Hershy looks around at him from time to time. Kaiser usually spurns his company, preferring to lie around the store or play with Max.

"The river's iced over solid," Sheldon says. "It's real good for sliding."

"Yeah? How d'ya know it'll hold ya?"

"It just does," says Sheldon.

At the river a knot of kids are sliding around near the base of the railroad bridge. Hershy and Sheldon slide down the bank of snow to join them. Kaiser picks his way down. Can this be the muddy Susquehanna lying bright and shining like a picture-book river!

Lorsh Jabieski and his sidekick Georgie are skating just as if they had real skates on. Hershy hardly ever sees his idol now that Lorsh goes to high school. Hershy has heard that Georgie's father was hurt in a rock fall last week and was buried in the mine for three-and-a-half hours. Now he can't work, even though the mines are busy. The paper says that the miners are trying to organize so that if men get hurt they can get some money. Now, Hershy figures, they probably have to get stuff from relief. He wonders, if something were to happen to his father—if the business fails as they worry it may—will they have to get food from barrels and old clothes from the relief?

Hershy slides onto the ice a couple of feet and slips around, struggling for balance. Nutty Cohen just sits on his tail on the ice. He can't seem to keep his balance. It is as if he has a weight in one pocket that keeps pulling him over.

Lenny Gorin is trying to organize a whip. Finally he gets half a dozen boys into a line and begins to lead them, each holding onto the other's waist, slipping and sliding downstream. After he leads them in a straight line for a few yards, Lenny turns suddenly, causing the whip to snap with much shouting and crashing and spills down the line. Lenny doubles up, howling, when Sheldon slides about ten feet across the ice on his belly, his glasses flying away from him.

"Sometime I'm goin' to bust him one," Sheldon says, retrieving his glasses.

Now Lenny is daring anyone to cross the river. He doesn't get any takers.

"Yer all yella," he says. "Everyone of ya. Even that big Polack." He gestures at Lorsh.

Sheldon looks nervously across the ice to Lorsh and Georgie, who appear not to hear. "You crazy?" he asks Lenny.

Hershy picks himself up from the ice, mad all over, and grabs Lenny by the collar. "Don't call them Polacks," he yells. "Stop calling them Polacks."

"Says who?" Lenny shakes Hershy off.

"You heard Rabbi Gold."

"Ah-h-h!" Lenny turns away. "Let's see who's got the guts to go across? Not one of ya is even willin' to try."

"Ah, why don't ya do it yourself," Morty says.

"I will when I feel like it," Lenny says.

"Yaaaa!" Morty gestures in disgust. "Yaaaa!"

Kaiser, it turns out, has made unsuccessful attempts to stand on the ice and his legs have slipped four ways from under him. He is now sprawled out and miserable. Hershy feels terrific rescuing Kaiser, really superior.

"I promised my father to help in the store this afternoon," he says to Sheldon. "I better go back."

Others are starting to leave, too. The original thrill is gone.

The store, which used to be in apple-pie order, is getting run down. Paint costs money, Mr. Marks says. New fixtures cost money. "I don't want to put money into it if we may have to . . . to give it up."

Mr. Marks is unpacking crates in the basement

and Hershy is minding the store. He takes poses of authority, standing behind the cash register, leaning nonchalantly on the counter. He doesn't really mind tending the store. He just doesn't want to do it for a living. He tries not to think about it, but he fears that it may be in his genes, that he is destined, somehow, to be a merchant, and something in him wishes this not to be true. But why? And what else is there for him to do in Ashlymine? And where else is there for him in the world? Choices do not seem to be there. Black hills hold him. These thoughts disturb him. He pushes them away and concentrates on the array of miners' equipment neatly lined up on the shelf across from the register. Caps, knee pads, lights, great round lunch pails with plenty of room for water at the bottom.

Then there are flame safety-lamps that would detect choke-damp, bad air. There are gas masks and carbon monoxide detectors. Mr. Marks says that a few of the old miners don't trust detectors and they still take canaries into the mines with them. If the canaries die, the miners know there is gas.

At least, Hershy thinks, he doesn't have that in his future. But that's probably Lorsh's future, down in the mines like his father. Long hours—that is, if you are lucky enough to work. And cold. Terrible wet cold.

Two boys enter the store and start browsing around. Hershy nods to them but stays quietly behind the counter. One of them paws through a box of marbles, looking long and longingly at the steel allies, at the big striped aggies. One looks at the display of dollar watches. They're Ingersolls and Hershy wouldn't mind having one himself.

"How much is this one?" he asks.

"They're all a dollar," Hershy says.

"Even this one?"

"All of them."

"How come they're all a dollar? Some are bigger than others."

Hershy shrugs. Mr. Marks appears in the back of the store.

"Okay. Dump your pockets," he shouts to the boy standing beside the box of marbles. "Dump them."

As Mr. Marks approaches, the boy cowers and empties his pockets. A dozen aggies and allies thunder onto the wooden floor.

"Out!" cries Mr. Marks. "And don't come back. That kind of customer we don't need. What's the matter—you can't keep your eye on business?" He looks disapprovingly at Hershy.

"I didn't see him, honest. I was lookin' at the watches the other kid was asking about."

"You've got to keep an eye on them all the time. Okay. You can go play now if you want."

Embarrassed at his failure, Hershy races around the counter and out the back door. Before he has gone fifty feet into the alley two hurtling forms drop him, their fists flying in Hershy's face, on his arms, head, chest. He tries to fight back, but the surprise attack has stunned him.

"That'll teach ya to blow the whistle, you *Zydek!*"

"I didn't blow the whistle," cries Hershy. "I didn't even know ya took stuff. Honest!" He receives a swat in the face for that. A parting kick and they are gone.

Hershy aches all over. He pulls himself over to the side of the alley, puts his hurt face down in a dirty snow pile. How could you be sorry for them? Where do you go for justice? Where? Where?

"Oh my God! What happened to you?" Mrs. Marks cries.

"I fell on the street," Hershy says.

"On your face?" asks Mr. Marks. Hershy shrugs.

Monday morning the sky is gray but there is a let-up in the cold snap. The walk up the hill is still hard labor over ice, but you can see it is easing up. The snow looks gray and dirty. Lenny isn't in school.

"He's run away again?" Hershy asks Sheldon at recess.

"I suppose so," Sheldon replies.

"I wonder what for, this time?" Hershy says.

"Bessie Gorin is near crazy," says Mrs. Marks that night. "He was away all Sunday. What a terrible kid that is, that Lenny. He gives them nothing but head-ache and heartache. He'll do that once too often and kill them."

During recess the next day at school, Mr. Ko-walski, the principal, calls Nutty, Morty, Sheldon, and Hershy to the office. Hershy is nervous. He sel-dom has occasion to talk with Mr. Kowalski, but when he does, it is usually about being late. Mr. Ko-walski looks like a prize fighter, not a school prin-cipal. Nobody horses around with him. He's tough. At the beginning of each school year, he assembles the students and puts the fear of God and Kowalski into them. He tells them that he is from the mines, himself, that he is the first person in his family to get a good education, and he appreciates it just like he wants them to appreciate it. He always ends with a combined warning and offer of peace.

"You play ball with me," he says, "and I'll play ball with you." You can tell by the way he says it that there is an "or else" in there somewhere. The four summoned to the office go with anxiety.

"What did we do?" asks Nutty.

"Dunno," Sheldon answers. "Nothin' that he should know anyway."

Mr. Kowalski is pacing around his office. An-other man in the room is standing by the window.

"Come in," the principal says. "Sit down."

The four, regarding Mr. Kowalski distrustfully, sit down on a bench.

"You're all friends of Lenny Gorin?" Mr. Kowalski asks.

"Yeah," Morty says. "Sort of."

Hershy is asking himself if Lenny is, indeed, his friend. The fact is he doesn't even like Lenny. But still, he's known him since they were small. They play ball together, they go to *cheder* together, they are both members of merchant families. They are stuck together by protective glue. Is that what a friend is? Hershy isn't sure.

"Lenny's missing," Mr. Kowalski says. "This is Detective Posanowski. He wants to ask you a few questions."

This is the first live detective any of them have ever seen. Hershy is disappointed. He is nothing at all like Nick Carter. Detective Posanowski is fat and short. He has a round face full of creases and pock marks. He wears a rumpled black suit and open galoshes that can't close over his fat ankles. He talks out of the side of his mouth, though, the way Hershy thinks detectives should. Or is that gangsters?

"When did you boys see Lenny last?" he asks.

"Down at the river on Saturday afternoon," Hershy says.

"What time was that?" Detective Posanowski asks.

The boys look at each other. Not one of them owns a watch, although all hope to get one this year as a *Bar Mitzvah* gift.

"Was it dark?" the detective asks.

"No," Hershy says. "It didn't get dark until after

I got home. I helped my father and then I went out and it was still not dark yet."

"Okay," says the detective. "Try and think if Lenny said anything about where he was going after that."

"He didn't say," Morty replies. "All he was sayin' was, 'I double-dare ya to cross the river.' Then we all went home."

"Even Lenny?"

The boys look at each other and shake their heads. Lenny hadn't been with them.

"When he dared you," says Detective Posanowski, "did he mean you should cross the ice?"

"Yeah," Morty says. "He's such a big mouth."

"He's just hidin' out, like always," Sheldon says. "Have ya looked in Grabowski's barn?"

"Yes, we have," the detective answers.

"Ya looked up at the Knob?" Nutty asks.

"Hasn't been anyone up to the Knob since the snow," the detective says. "No footprints there at all."

Hershy is impressed. Despite his appearance, Detective Posanowski is talking just like a detective.

"That's all, I guess," Detective Posanowski nods at Mr. Kowalski.

"Thank you, boys," Mr. Kowalski says.

As they walk back to their classroom, Hershy thinks that talking to the principal, if you haven't done anything wrong, isn't so bad. He also notes that, even though Detective Posanowski is a Polack—

a Polish person—he is really trying hard to find out what has happened to Lenny. But that's his job, isn't it? You can't really tell how he feels about it.

Lenny has never hidden out this long before. Two weeks go by and the cold snap is over. The snow turns to slush. And then the four boys are called once again to Mr. Kowalski's office. He has them sit down on the bench.

"I'm very sad to be the one to tell you this, boys, but I didn't want you to hear it as sensational gossip. I'm afraid the hunt for Lenny is over. He's been found. He's been found . . . dead."

Hershy can't believe what he is hearing. It is like a book. It will turn out to be a mistake.

"He was drowned . . . probably that Saturday on the ice. The body washed up across the river in Nanticoke. He must have fallen through the ice when everyone else had left." He looks closely at the stunned boys. "I'm sorry, very sorry, boys. I know what it is to lose a friend. I've lost some myself . . . in the mines."

"He did it!" Sheldon says as they walk down the hall. "He actually walked across the river, the nut!"

"Don't call him a nut," Morty says. "He's dead."

Dead. Hershy is trying to get it through his head. Old people he has known have died and he has been sorry. But someone his own age! It is hard to understand. He remembers how he felt when Mr. Weeks, the manual arts teacher, died. Hershy had such a hard time realizing he would never see him again. He would go to class and see things Mr. Weeks had made—patterns of wood, a footstool, a birdhouse, a salt box. He would see all the tools Mr. Weeks had used, all the lumber, but not Mr. Weeks. *He would never see him again!* He will never see Lenny again. It makes him feel strange—scared, more than anything.

As soon as Hershy comes through the door Mrs. Marks swoops down on him and embraces him. This is not her usual greeting. Hershy holds himself stiffly and allows himself to be enveloped. Then Mrs. Marks grabs him by the shoulders and starts to shake him and yell, "Were you walking on the ice, too? I know you were! Don't you ever let me hear about you going out on the ice again! Do you hear me? Never, never, never! What are you trying to do, send me to the grave?"

She stops shaking him and Hershy sees that her eyes are all blurry and red. Now her voice comes down an octave.

"All right. Take the garbage down now, but come right back."

IX

thieves and trouble

THEY ARE standing on the roof of Wise's Dry Goods. It's a terrific roof—very flat—and some years ago Mr. Wise had marked out a shuffle board on the tar paper. It has faded in the rains and snows, and coal dust has blended it with the tar paper background, but traces remain. The roof gives them a view of the town all the way down the hill to the river and up over the roofs to the school. They have an over-view of Market Street in front, and a view of the alley in back.

It is the alley that draws their attention now as four Polish boys come swinging down, laughing and poking each other. On impulse, Morty reaches down into the gutter of the roof where the water drains,

114

picks up a good-sized pebble, and heaves it through the air. Quite marvelously, it hits Jim Romanski right in the shoulder. The other boys on the roof gasp and Sheldon ducks down behind the parapet. But Nutty, inspired by Morty's example, grabs a pebble and throws it, and Morty reaches for another. Hershy just stands there, caught between the thought of joining Sheldon in safety, the desire to watch the war, and the urge to participate in a strike against the enemy.

The Poles are reaching for bigger rocks in the alley and aiming them at the roof. Most fall short, but some fall onto the tar paper. And then one crashes through a back window. Mrs. Wise's head appears in the window and Mr. Wise comes storming out the back door.

"Hoodlums! *Gonifs!*" yells Mr. Wise.

The Poles beat it down the alley and the boys on the roof sink down and lean against the parapet. Morty and Nutty are clapping each other on the back.

"We got 'em for once!" Morty cries. "We got 'em."

"That's what you think," Sheldon says. He gets up to leave. "You think they're not gonna get even?"

"Ah, they get even when we don't do anything at all," Morty says as they go down through the roof hatch and into the house. "Hey Hersh, wanna hang around for a game of cards?"

. . .

As usual, Morty cheats at rummy, but Hershy is used to it. He just throws him a disgusted look every once in a while.

"Come on, Hersh! It's more fun if ya bet some money—even a cent or a nickel."

"Got no money," Hershy says. He isn't going to bet so much as a baseball card with Morty.

They are sitting on the floor of the store, now closed for the day. Morty is leaning against a bin of oatmeal cookies. Every few minutes he pops open the glass top of the bin and takes a cookie.

"Want one?" he asks Hershy.

"I've had enough," Hershy says. In fact, he knows he can eat another six, but he feels too guilty eating Mr. Wise's merchandise.

Morty lays an ace and a two on his three-card meld, then draws three cards from the pack and inspects them.

"Whoops! Only need two," he says, and puts one back. "How come nobody around here seems to know how to get hold of any dough except me?"

Morty always seems to have plenty of change. Hershy doesn't know where he gets it.

"Play!" commands Morty.

Hershy lays down the two, three, four of hearts, and three kings.

"How'd ya do that?" Morty is stunned. It is bad enough to be beaten anytime. He takes it hard. But he can't figure out how Hershy can beat him when he, Morty, is cheating.

"Ya must have cheated," Morty decides.

"Not me," Hershy says.

Morty gets up and goes over to the icebox. He opens the door and stares into it in the special kind of trance that comes over people before an open icebox door. Staring and looking for inspiration, he reaches into the butter tub with his fingers and captures a chunk of sweet butter which he smears on a roll. Then he dips the roll into the sugar bin. He offers Hershy a bite, but Hershy shakes his head, though he is drooling. Morty climbs up and lies down on the counter.

"My father says I should be a lawyer when I grow up," he says. "I dunno, though. I think it's a lot of work, and once I get out of high school, I don't know if I wanna do anymore of that kind of work. I'm not so hot in school, ya know. But my pa thinks I am. How about you?"

"I guess you're okay."

"Nah. I mean what d'ya wanna be?"

Hershy tries to ignore the question. He doesn't have to make decisions like that, does he?

"Hersh? What about you? What d'ya wanna be, huh?"

Now the question is squarely put and there is no dodging it. Hershy feels pretty bad.

"Dunno," he says.

"Well, ya *gotta* know," Morty insists. "Everybody's gotta be something. If I'm a lawyer," he goes on, "I won't have to worry about being unemployed.

My father says lawyers are never unemployed."

"Even now in the Depression?" Hershy asks.

"Even in the Depression, because guys still rob banks and all, and other guys still sue people."

Hershy can't remember anything except the Depression, although his father has told him there were plenty of years when Hershy was younger that things were really good. They had built the store, a really nice building of red brick, and there was plenty of everything, his father said. In those days, though the miners were never prosperous, they paid their bills sooner or later, and they didn't hesitate so long to buy something they needed. And the merchants, too, bought things extravagantly from one another. But then came the Crash of 1929. The bottom fell out of the stock market. Hershy isn't sure what that means, but he knows that all over the country there are people who are poor now who were never poor before. Here in the Valley just last week, the relief workers distributed seven hundred barrels of free flour to needy families, along with recipes for baking bread. And people are always collecting clothing for the poor. Hershy wonders who "the poor" are. In Ashlymine it is hard to tell because nobody seems to have any money, not even the storekeepers.

"So what d'ya think, Hersh? What d'ya want to be?"

Hershy struggles with the verb "to be." The comfortable sense of "I am" is slipping from him, leaving him lonely. Yet something that must have been under the surface begins to appear like invisible ink made of lemon juice.

"One thing I know," he says slowly, as the writing becomes clearer. "I don't wanna be in the hardware business." But still, the necessity of choice hangs heavily on him.

When Hershy returns home he interrupts a loud conversation. His mother is pushing dough into a noodle machine and raising her voice over the clatter of the grinding handle.

"Face it, Lou. Either you've got to get the money from the people that owe you, or you've got to borrow, or else we've got *tsuris*." Then she sees Hershy.

"Aha, you're here! Take down the garbage."

"But it's nearly empty."

"Take it down, anyway."

Hershy learned long ago not to argue points of logic or practice with his mother. She can outmaneuver him. He takes the garbage can down the stairs, going down two and back one step to be unique. Kaiser pushes down the stairs past Hershy, knocking him off balance, and spilling the contents of the can. He has to spend some time picking it up.

When he returns, his mother and father are still at it. Kaiser goes in and sits down, but Hershy waits quietly in the doorway. Mr. Marks is hunched over lists and bills, shaking his head.

"I'm going to squeeze money out of coal?" he

asks. "These people haven't worked more than a couple of weeks, for months. How am I going to ask them for money? If I ask them, how are they going to pay me?"

Mrs. Marks shrugs. "So, that's what I say. You have to borrow it."

"Where am I going to borrow three hundred dollars?"

"The bank."

"The bank. They already have a mortgage on this store. Should I borrow from the bank to pay the mortgage to the bank? Is that what you're telling me to do?"

"All right, then, my sister Milly."

"No! I don't want to ask her."

"You don't have to. I will."

"It's the same thing."

"She's got plenty of money and it wouldn't hurt her to help someone in the family for a change."

"We always made out without help."

"You want to lose the store? Look around you. Did you ever think Morris Pearl would go out of business? Did you? And I happen to know that Wise is having a hard time and may have to close. And then what? What do they do then? What would we do?"

Hershy is statue still, but inside his heart is bursting. Does this mean they are poor? Will he have to pick coal with the Grabowski kids, with Lorsh Jabieski's kid brother? Is his family now like the miners' families—like Lorsh's family—down on their luck? *Now* is he in the same boat as they? Is he a member of that society, too, part of that large accepted group—"the poor"?

Mr. Marks is shaking his head. "I still don't like the idea," he says.

Hershy steps into the room. "I'll turn the handle for ya," he says, taking over the noodle machine. His mother continues to feed the dough. As shapeless dough is transformed into delicious slivers, the noodles come out the other end. Max walks in from the bedroom and grabs some.

"Don't eat raw dough. How many times do I have to tell you?" Mrs. Marks raises her voice and her hand. Max ducks. He is charmed, Hershy thinks. If it were he, the smack would have connected.

Coming into the store the next afternoon, Hershy finds his mother standing at the front counter.

"Don't bother Pop," she whispers. "Someone is in the back talking to him about maybe buying the store."

"But he can't sell the store! Where would we live?" Hershy whispers anxiously.

Mrs. Marks closes her eyes. "One thing at a time. He hasn't sold it yet."

A staccato of voices emerges from the back of the store. Then the prospective buyer speaks loudly. "You'll see," he says. "You won't get another offer as good. Here's my number. Call me if you change your mind." And he turns and strides out.

Through the window Hershy can see him going to his car, which is parked down the street. He climbs in but doesn't start the car. Mr. Marks, looking discouraged, goes behind the counter to straighten some stock.

"Maybe I should have taken it?" he ventures.

"No. You were right," says Mrs. Marks. "It isn't enough."

Hershy sits in the window with Kaiser beside him. He keeps his eyes on the old Buick parked down the street. Why is the car staying there? After about ten minutes, the door on the passenger side opens and a fat man gets out. He leans down and speaks through the window to the man inside. Then he turns and comes across the street towards the Markses' store. He is coming in.

"Good afternoon," he says, as he opens the door. "I hear by the grapevine that your shop is for sale. I've come to make you an offer."

Mr. Marks looks optimistic. "Welcome," he says, and he shows the man around. But in a few minutes they emerge from the back of the shop and the man leaves.

"If you got that kind of offer," he says as he goes out, "I would advise you to take it. I can't match that."

"It sounds like I should have taken the first

offer," Mr. Marks says. "This man isn't offering nearly as much."

"But Pop," Hershy says.

"Hush," says Mrs. Marks. "This is grown-up business."

"But Pop . . ."

"The first man said I wouldn't get as good an offer. He's right."

"But Pop." Hershy doesn't wait this time for permission to interrupt. "Both those men came out of the same car. Why would he offer less when ya won't give it to his friend for more? Those men are together."

"How do you know?" Mr. Marks asks sharply. "Are you sure?"

"I've been watching them. I wondered why the first man didn't start the car. I thought it might be stuck."

"The crook!" shouts Mrs. Marks. "The *gonif!* He sent his friend to underbid so you'd take his cheap offer." She clenches her fist.

"You're a smart boy," Mr. Marks says. "Keep up like that and you'll do okay."

Mrs. Marks sees it as an omen that they should go and ask Aunt Milly.

Nutty and Hershy are hurrying to *cheder.* They have just turned the corner when a monster with many strong arms drags them into an alley and then into someone's backyard. Hershy, now lying on the ground, looks up and sees that the arms belong to Jim Romanski, Tom Grabowski, Georgie, and Lorsh. And *Lorsh!*

"Where's the other one?" asks Jim, poking Hershy with his foot.

Hershy doesn't answer. Jim prods him again with his foot, harder this time. "Where's the other guy who chucked the rocks?"

"I dunno," Hershy mumbles. Then he looks straight at Lorsh and says, "I didn't chuck rocks."

"Oh yeah!" Jim laughs. "I suppose them stones just flew by themselves." All the Poles laugh. Lorsh, too.

"Come on! We don't have all day," Tom says. "Let's do it."

Hershy feels himself begin to quiver as he sees lengths of clothesline being pulled down from the T-shaped poles in the yard.

"Hurry up or they'll see us," Tom hisses to Georgie.

"There's no one home," Lorsh says. "This house is empty in the daytime."

They begin by tying Nutty to the clothes pole. Then they stretch his arms out and tie them to the cross bars. Hurriedly, they do the same for Hershy. His feet just touch the ground. His arms are stretched to their fullest. The wind is blowing across the yard and cuts their faces. When Hershy tries to turn and see what else the Poles may be up to, he finds they have gone.

Nutty is whimpering. Hershy doesn't cry but he's mortified, disappointed, and scared. They could be here all night and freeze. They could die here. The blood seems to have left his arms. His wrists hurt where the ropes are cutting. His armpits pain where his arms are overstretched. His neck aches as it strains forward. And they have missed *cheder!* Darkness starts to fall. Only then it occurs to him to yell, and he yells.

"Oh my God!" The woman who lives in the house has come home, carrying groceries, and found them. She drops her packages, runs into the house, and comes out with a kitchen knife. The knife scares Hershy as she wields it, but she doesn't draw blood. She has cut them down in a few minutes. Hershy sees they have been freed by a Polish lady. But she is yelling.

"Look at you! Look at my clothesline! What is this, some game?"

Hershy nods. He finds he can't talk.

"Kids!" she says. "You're all alike!"

X

gifts

THE OLD Dodge is having trouble on the last stretch before the big descent into Easton. It has been a tiring dusty ride through the bad roads of the Pocono Mountains, the engine overheating on every steep hill. Every time they stop to let it cool off Hershy makes small expeditions into the piney woods at the side of the road, followed by Max yelling, "Wait for me! Wait for me!" Their trips out of the Valley have been so few that any kind of excursion is important. Down a grassy slope and at the edge of an icy-cold creek, Hershy feels the great force of water touch his hands. How can there be so much power in such shallow water?

"You hold onto Max!" Mrs. Marks shouts. "Don't slip. Watch out for the wet rocks. Come on back. It's cool now."

A few hours earlier Mr. Marks put a sign up in the store announcing that it would be closed this afternoon and tomorrow. As he did every night, he left the cash register drawer open. This was to prevent any possible burglar from forcing it and doing expensive damage. And, although the store has never been burglarized, the drawer was always left full of pennies to assure that this burglar, whoever he may be, will not be entirely disappointed and therefore tempted to steal something valuable or to vandalize the store. As a further precaution Kaiser was locked inside to guard the premises. He was left with his dinner, and Mr. Wise was going in to walk him and feed him tomorrow.

Long famous for losing his way, Mr. Marks wasted an hour on the wrong turnings, so that the trip was longer than it needed to be.

Now Max sleeps in the back seat of the car and the rest of the family put all their efforts into making the final climb. Hershy leans forward, shoulders hunched, teeth clenched, eyes squinting, pushing with his will. Mrs. Marks is clutching the seat and grunting a little. Mr. Marks, his foot down to the floorboard, is rocking back and forth as if the car were a horse. Max sleeps on. A great exhalation of relief pushes the car over the brow of the hill. Then, Mr. Marks focuses his eyes on the roller-coaster descent, foot tapping the brake, arms rigid, guiding the Dodge down the great hill into Easton.

"Do you think Sam and Belle got your letter that we're coming?" Mr. Marks asks his wife, when he can relax.

"I didn't send it."

"You didn't send it!"

"I didn't want them to go to any extra trouble."

"You don't think it's trouble if we come without telling them?"

"What trouble? They put a couple of blankets on the floor for the kids, and we use their kids' room."

"What's this big place here?" Hershy asks.

"That's a college," Mr. Marks answers. "Lafayette College."

"Do they teach ya to be a lawyer there?"

"I don't know," Mr. Marks says. "Who's going to be a lawyer?"

"Maybe Morty," Hershy replies.

"That *gonif!*" Mr. Marks exclaims. "He can be his own client. The kid's a crook already. Steals from his father's register."

"How d'ya know?" Hershy is stunned.

"Wise told me. He's waiting to catch him red-handed and then he's going to teach him a lesson."

So that's where Morty gets his money! Hershy is horrified. He thinks about warning Morty that his father knows. And then how would Morty feel if he knew that Hershy knows? Morty doesn't believe things until they happen, anyway. Like he didn't believe the teacher when she said she'd keep him after school for a week if he copied from Sarah Pomerantz anymore. But he did and she did.

The car winds around some streets before it pulls up in front of a brown shingle house with a porch.

"Is this Aunt Milly's house?" asks Max. He always wakes as soon as the car stops—as if the engine runs his sleep machinery.

"No," Mrs. Marks answers. "This is Easton. Aunt Milly lives across the bridge in Phillipsburg. This is your Uncle Sam's place. We're going to stay here tonight and see Aunt Milly in the morning."

As they climb out, the car seems to relax with a sigh. Hershy thinks that it sags like the milkman's tired horse which shifts its weight from one foot to the other, seeking a comfortable position.

Mrs. Marks rings the bell. "Anyone home?" she calls in a pleasant yodel. "Yoo hoo. Anyone home?"

The door is opened by her brother's wife, Belle, who regards them open-mouthed. She says nothing —she's that surprised—but Mrs. Marks fills the silence by crying, "Look who's here! Hello, hello! Surprised? Where's Sam? Look, here's Lou and Hershy and Max, too. Let's come on in, everybody!"

Although Aunt Belle is surprised, she does not seem put out. She sends her Mimmy and Joan to the grocery for more bread before the store closes, and then hurries into the kitchen to see what she can put together for supper. Uncle Sam hugs everyone and says that, first thing in the morning, he will take Hershy and Max down to the newspaper where he works as a pressman and show them how the great presses work.

Supper is exactly the same as it might have been at home—cold meat, cold peas, a *kugel,* and some sponge cake.

"I wish I'd known you were coming. I would have had a hot meal," mourns Aunt Belle.

"See!" Mrs. Marks says. "What did I tell you! If I'd let them know, she would have gone to a lot of trouble." Mr. Marks smiles weakly and nods his head rapidly, then shrugs. Hershy knows that this is his recognition of his wife's better judgment.

"How's Milly?" Mrs. Marks asks.

"Oh, you know Milly," Aunt Belle answers. "She never changes. You'd think there wasn't anyone else in the world. You'd never even think there was a Depression. She has no idea what's going on. All she does is crochet and talk to that old halfwit Mary who looks after her. I never believed that you and Sam and Milly were sisters and brother."

"She's a half-sister, you know, and she's a lot older," Mrs. Marks says. "Like another generation."

"And a lot richer," says Sam. "A lot richer."

"She just married lucky," Mrs. Marks says. Hershy thinks his father looks sad or embarrassed. "I'm going to see her tomorrow," Mrs. Marks continues.

"Enjoy yourself," Aunt Belle replies. "Enjoy yourself."

"So what's new?" Mr. Marks asks his brother-in-law. Everyone listens to him because he works on the newspaper.

"I saw on the news service wire, just before I left today, that all the Jewish stores in some town in Germany were raided and the merchants arrested by the Nazis," he said.

"It can't be," says Mr. Marks, putting down his fork. "Why would they do that?"

"Why would they do that! Why would they do any of the things that have been going on—arresting Jewish doctors, firing teachers. Even Einstein resigned from the Academy of Science because of what they are doing. In this day and age! Can you believe it!"

Hershy is confused. "I only read the French are afraid Hitler is going to start a war," he breaks in.

"Because we're not getting the *New York Times* now that the salesman isn't stopping anymore," Mr. Marks says. "The *Record* doesn't tell as much about some things."

"What will happen?" Hershy asks. "Will anyone stop it?" His voice is breaking, high to low, low to high, but he has no time for embarrassment.

"Who knows!" says Uncle Sam, shaking his head. "Who knows!"

"But could that happen . . . what you said . . . to the stores in Ashlymine?"

"No," Uncle Sam answers.

"How come? We have trouble, too."

"It's not the same," Uncle Sam says.

"Why not?"

"Hershy!" Mr. Marks says sharply. "Not now. No more of your questions."

"Pop, *I wanna know the answer.*"

Mr. Marks turns his palms up, empty. He shakes his head and speaks softly, "Hersh, we don't know the answer."

Hershy and Max haven't seen their cousins Mimmy and Joan for four years. Then they had come to Ashlymine for his parents' tenth anniversary. There'd been a real party with dozens of sponge cakes, honey cakes, fruit, and dancing the *hora* for hours till everyone dropped. Hardware had rattled in the shop below. Even though it was late November, Hershy and Max slept on the sleeping porch so that Mimmy and Joan could use their room. But under featherbeds, great deep puffs his grandmother had brought from the old country, it was warm and comfortable. Hershy plans to sleep out on the porch this year until it gets too cold to stand—maybe all winter. That way he can have a room for himself.

Now, in Aunt Belle's living room, Max, of course, falls asleep on two chairs pushed together for a bed. Joan is given the couch. Hershy is told to put his blankets on the floor behind the couch, and Mimmy in front. When everyone is settled for the night, Mimmy crawls around the couch and shines her flashlight on Hershy.

"Wanna trade movie cards?" she asks.

"Sure," he says.

"Sh-h-h!" She holds up a warning finger. "Whisper." Then she throws a pack of cards three inches thick onto the floor and kneels down.

Never without something to trade, Hershy reaches for his windbreaker and pulls out a pack. "Okay," he says. "What d'ya have?"

"Greta Garbo," she says. "What'll ya give me?"

"I don't want it. I hate her."

"Greta Garbo! Why?" Hershy shrugs. Mimmy says, "Okay, Norma Shearer."

"Okay," says Hershy. "My Norma Shearer got wet. I'll give ya a John Barrymore or a John Gilbert."

"I got them both. Ya got Tom Mix?"

"Yeah, but I don't trade Tom Mix. I keep 'em. I got one hundred and fifty Tom Mixes."

This is the first time he has done any trading with a girl and he is surprised. She is a good trader. He remembers four years ago when she was a nag and a pain in the neck.

He finally gets the Norma Shearer, a Hoot Gibson, and a Ken Maynard. Mimmy says she has to get up early and go to the store for fresh rolls, so she better go to sleep.

"Okay," Hershy says. "Good night."

"Night," she replies.

He lies awake a few minutes thinking. He has had just as good a time trading with her as with Sheldon or Morty. It's sort of surprising.

After an early breakfast, Uncle Sam takes Hershy and Max down to the newspaper to watch the big presses, just as he promised. Hershy thinks he has never seen anything quite so magnificent—rolls of paper as big as a sewer pipe slip through the enormous cylinders of the presses and come out as newspapers, all folded, just the way they arrive at the house. So that's how a newspaper is made. The smell of the fresh ink is as good as *kugel,* in its own way. The linotype machines that set the type perform some sort of magic, putting all the letters down in rows that always come out even. And the reporters sit at their desks poking out the news stories on big noisy typewriters! These are the same kind of stories he reads every day about politics, about crime, the mines, even about Europe and the whole world.

A light bulb turns on in Hershy's head, just like in the comics.

"Now, *that's* what I wanna do when I grow up," Hershy announces.

"What?" asks Uncle Sam.

"Anything around here," Hershy says, feeling his future is settled. What could be more a part of the real world! It takes a real load off his mind.

Mrs. Marks has brought the boys' good clothes and, when they come back from the newspaper, she

sees that Hershy and Max change and that their
shoes are tied carefully, their socks neatly turned,
and their knickers at even heights.

"Where's Pop?" Hershy asks, as they start the
ten-block walk. His good shoes seem a lot tighter
than the last time he wore them.

"His back hurt this morning from all that driv-
ing, so I told him to stay in bed and take it easy. He'll
just have to miss seeing Aunt Milly."

They are approaching the bridge over the Delaware River and Mrs. Marks is walking fast and talking fast. "Be polite," she says to the boys. "Don't say
anything unless she speaks right to you. Don't touch
anything. Aunt Milly is very nervous. She's been sick
and she's not used to children. I don't see how she
can even enjoy her money because she can't eat. She
has something the matter with her stomach, so don't
upset her."

"Entering New Jersey," a sign says in the middle
of the bridge. Hershy has walked from one state to
another without any effort and hardly noticing the
difference.

Mrs. Marks stops to straighten the ties of both
boys before they climb the steps to the big brick
house. A round woman in slippers answers the door-
bell.

"Is my sister at home?" asks Mrs. Marks.

"Who is it, Mary?" a whiney voice calls from the
house.

"It's Fanny," Mrs. Marks calls, putting her head

in the door. "May we come in? I have the boys with me." She pushes Mary firmly aside and ushers the boys through the dark hallway and into the even darker sitting room beyond.

Like the memory of a dream, Hershy recalls the room, dark with its black tapestry on matched carved chairs and sofa. He hasn't been here since he was Max's age. He remembers Aunt Milly as being deaf, but he is not entirely sure because although she did not answer questions, she was always telling him to stop sniffing.

Mrs. Marks is being very agreeable, talking of the ride from Ashlymine, asking about Aunt Milly's health. Finally she gets to the point.

"Milly," she begins. "You know how I hate asking for anything . . ."

Aunt Milly isn't paying attention. She is looking all over the room. "You see that piece of thread over there on the carpet. Pick it up. Nobody said you were coming," she complains to Mrs. Marks. Hershy picks up the thread.

"I wanted to surprise you," Mrs. Marks says. She talks louder, trying to get Aunt Milly's interest. "It's Lou," she says.

"How's Lou?" Aunt Milly asks, as if she had raised the subject herself.

"He's in good health, thank God," says Mrs. Marks. "Except, sometimes, a little short of breath. It's the anxiety. He's worried about the store. The mines are just starting to work again, you know. Peo-

ple don't pay their bills yet. Lou has to pay the
mortgage on the store. He has to pay the suppliers
so we can get stock. We just need a little help to tide
us over. Lou says things are going to be better now
that Roosevelt's in."

"Was it very cold up there in March?" asks Aunt
Milly.

"Not too cold. We had a cold snap in February,
so the mines were working for a little while. Listen,
Milly, we want to ask if you can let us have . . .
maybe . . . well, three hundred dollars for a little
while. Just until people pay."

"It was terribly cold here. We must have burned
twice the coal we used to. Old Len—he takes care of
the furnace—took sick and sometimes he couldn't
come to stoke it or bank it or whatever he does."

Hershy is getting a terrible itch from sitting on
the prickly sofa. He can feel it through his pants.

"Don't scratch," Aunt Milly says.

Max has fallen asleep. Hershy wishes he had
Max's talent for instant sleep.

Mrs. Marks now raises her voice and talks directly into Aunt Milly's face.

"Milly! *Listen, will you!* I've come all the way from
Ashlymine just to see you about this."

"Don't shout," Aunt Milly says. "I'm glad to see
you, Fanny. You don't come very often."

"Milly, Lou needs . . ."

"You tell Lou not to worry. There have been
hard times before. I remember in 1918 you couldn't

get any sugar at all. All the men away in the army or navy. It always gets better. Just tell him to hold on. That's what my Morris always told everyone. Just trim a little here and trim a little there and you'll get by, you'll see."

Aunt Milly seems much cheerier than when they came in. She sits back in her chair and resumes the crocheting she put down when they arrived. Mrs. Marks stands up and pulls at her dress and tugs at her stockings. She stares hard at Aunt Milly for a second and then she turns, signaling Hershy. Hershy nudges Max and drags him to his feet.

"You going so soon?" whines Aunt Milly. "You just got here. Don't you want some *kuchen* and coffee?"

Hershy wants some *kuchen,* but Mrs. Marks shakes her head. "No, thank you, Milly. We'll have to be starting back to Ashlymine soon. It's a long way to go, you know." They move towards the hallway.

"Oh, just a minute, Fanny. I have something for you."

Hershy sees a spark of light in his mother's eyes. She raises her head in half-hope. Perhaps Aunt Milly has just been teasing them.

Aunt Milly pulls herself painfully to her feet and moves like a wound-up mechanical toy across the room to a chest in the hallway.

"Open that chest, boy," she snaps. Hershy lifts the lid of the heavy old carved chest. Aunt Milly bends down, rummages around, and then takes

something from the dark interior. She extends her
arm to Mrs. Marks. In her hand is a long fur-piece
made up of several orangey animals biting each
other's tails. What had they been! Hershy wonders.

"You can have this," says Aunt Milly. "I don't go
out much any more."

Mrs. Marks looks confused as she extends her
hand to accept the fur-piece. She mutters something
that Hershy can't understand, then turns sharply,
and pushes Hershy and Max out the door.

Then they begin the forced double-time march,
down the streets towards the bridge to Easton. Mrs.
Marks sets the pace, walking ahead with the fur-
piece held in front of her, her arm in exactly the
position it was in when she received the gift. Hershy
is stepping fast, and Max has to run to keep up with
them. Hershy never knew his mother could walk this
fast. But she seems dazed, like a very fast sleep-
walker. She is muttering to herself.

"She never had anything and then she had a lot.
Now she holds onto every last thing, even when she
doesn't need it."

"Maybe she didn't hear ya right," Hershy says,
trying to release his mother from the tight bonds of
anger that seem to strap her voice tightly in her
throat and keep her face stiff and her eyes staring.
Max keeps calling, "Wait for me, wait for me," and
running on his fat legs.

"She heard, all right," Mrs. Marks says. "She

hears every word. She just picks out what she wants to understand. She—she—" They are crossing the big bridge over the Delaware River now and are nearly across on the upstream side of the bridge. Suddenly Mrs. Marks turns, her arms still stiff in front of her, and leaning out over the abutment, deliberately drops the fur-piece over the railing. She stares after it, still in a trance, and Hershy, stunned, stares, too.

Then, quite as suddenly, Mrs. Marks snaps out of her sleepwalking phase, lets out a wail, and then yells in a voice that Hershy recognizes as normal, "Hershy, quick! Run down the bank under the bridge and grab it. It must be worth something."

The wail and the shout attract the attention of a few people crossing the bridge, who run to the railing to see if someone has fallen over or jumped. Hershy slips and slides down the bank. The fur-piece can be seen bobbing on the slow river just out of reach. The people on the bridge are pointing. "A dog . . . a cat," are words in the air. Hershy grabs for something—a big broken branch—and reaches as far as he can, nearly touching the furry flotsam. Then, a little current of water whirls the fur-piece out of reach and it slips by him. It hits a rock, whirls in a little eddy, and disappears. A sigh goes up on the bridge. "It's gone, poor thing. Was it yours?" the onlookers ask Mrs. Marks.

Mrs. Marks grabs Max's hand and pulls him to

the other side of the bridge, where they wait for Hershy to climb the bank.

"Hurry," she says. Tears are streaming down her face. Hershy cannot remember ever having seen his mother cry like this before. It is awesome.

When they arrive back at Aunt Belle's Mrs. Marks has stopped crying but her eyes are still quite red and blotchy. As soon as they enter the house, she throws her arms around Mr. Marks's neck and says, "Oh, Lou! What're we going to do now?"

Hershy is stunned and unsettled. Here she is— Queen of the Black Iron Stove, the Organizer of All of Them, the Director of His Life—now as weak as he, himself, sometimes feels.

Also, it surprises and embarrasses him to see his father embracing his mother just like in the movies. A pat on the shoulder, a peck good night is all he has witnessed before. So real people act like that, even his mother and father!

"What's the matter, Fanny?" asks Mr. Marks, in a voice he might use to address a child. "Did she eat one of the kids?" His idea of a joke. He pokes her under the chin and looks at her streaked face.

And there, Hershy thinks, is his father, the quiet accepter of life as it happens, almost like another child to his mother, now taking charge and treating her as a child. It is confusing.

"Cheer up! All the trouble's over for now," says

Mr. Marks. "Belle and Sam are lending us the money."

"Why didn't you tell us about all this before?" asks Uncle Sam.

"How can they lend us the money? Where . . ."

"Oh, we've saved a little. I've got a steady job," says Uncle Sam. "Why shouldn't I invest in a family business. You'll pay it back sometime. Don't worry. If not, I guess I'll own part of a hardware store in Ashlymine." He laughs.

To make things more confusing, Mrs. Marks cries even harder now. Hershy gives up trying to figure it out. He has a strong wish to go and pat his mother's shoulder, but he doesn't. He sits quietly feeling this big family, which he is a part of, taking him in.

an end/a beginning

HERSHY'S TONE-DEAF ear is doing him dirt. He looks to heaven for help and aims his voice at a note in the general direction of the ceiling. Any note, something up there.

"No, Herschel, like this," and the rabbi chants one of the lines that Hershy is trying to learn. His *Bar Mitzvah* is to be next Saturday and he has been working for weeks on this assigned reading from the Torah, the passage that would normally be read by the rabbi on that particular day. Hershy has all the words down pat, all the difficult Hebrew sentences committed to memory. He has worked on them in every spare moment. But this chanting has got him in a sweat. He has memorized his address to the

143

congregation, too: "Beloved parents, esteemed rabbi, dear friends, and worthy members of the congregation, today I am a man . . ."

His mother has been baking for a week. The house is already full of *kugel,* sponge cakes, angel cakes, strudel, *rugelah,* honey cakes, raisin cakes, and nut cakes. Max is sticky all the time from putting his fingers into batters. You can hardly sit down because there is a yeast cake rising under blankets or coats on nearly all the chairs. His father has brought up a jug of sweet wine from the cellar. It is a rare treat and is usually kept for Passover and other holy days. Glasses have been polished and two cut-glass bowls stand ready to hold fruit. All the relatives from Easton are coming and all the friends from around Ashlymine. Mr. Marks is worried that the building might be too undermined to hold so many people. The excitement, Hershy finds, is killing. The attention, though flattering, is beginning to weigh heavily.

"Try again," Rabbi Gold says, tapping Hershy on the shoulder to get his entire attention. "From the beginning."

Hershy chants the whole passage now, imagining himself standing at the altar in his new ceremonial shawl and cap, the eyes of the congregation on him, his parents, no doubt, praying—praying he will make no mistakes.

"Okay," Rabbi Gold says, giving him a clap on the back. "You'll do. Just take my advice, don't try to get a job as a cantor."

Hershy hurries home. These rehearsals keep him late at the *shul*. His mother gets nervous when she has to give him supper after everyone else is through and she has already started something like rolling out cookies on the kitchen table. But by the end of the week, this will be all over. As he approaches the store he can see the dark shape of a person peering through the glass. The dark shape brightens as he gets closer. At first he doesn't believe it, but it is Lorsh Jabieski. He stops short. He still has bad feelings about the clothes-pole incident—anger and disappointment.

"Store closed?" Lorsh asks, just as if this is something that happens all the time.

"Uh, I guess so," Hershy says. Why is it that he can only look at his hands and feet? What he wants to do is tell him off. What he wants to say is who does he think he is. No, what he wants to say is that he didn't *need* to do it, that . . .

"Heck! I need some carbide."

Now Hershy looks up. There are streaks of coal dust on Lorsh's face. He is wearing heavy steel-toed miner's boots. A kind of sadness hits Hershy for a moment and then he suddenly comes to life and starts to move.

"I can get some for ya. Wait." He is already streaking around the store and up the backstairs into the cake-filled kitchen. His mother calls, "Now where are you running!" Down the inside stairs into the shop is where he is running. He pries open the corrugated can of carbide and scoops some into a brown paper bag and weighs it on the scale. It is a generous measure. Then he unlocks the shop door and hands the bag to Lorsh.

"How much?" Lorsh asks.

"Just exactly a quarter's worth," Hershy says.

"Can I charge it?"

"Sure," Hershy says. "Sure. I'll write it on the books." He feels like a big shot for just a minute.

"Well thanks," Lorsh says. "S'long."

"S'long," Hershy says. "S'long."

And then he is stricken! Now Lorsh owes him money! He is in debt to the store. Hershy wants to call him back. He wants to run after Lorsh and say the carbide is a gift. A gift from a friend. Can he do that? He could run and overtake him; he knows that. But can he keep the cycle from beginning? Can he make things *not* happen? Can he stop the force that makes things the way they are?

"Hershy! I've been calling you!" Mrs. Marks has her head out the living room window above the store entrance. Hershy remains rooted. "Hershy! Rabbi Gold is on the phone for you."

"For me!" Hershy can't imagine the rabbi calling him. He slams and locks the store door and takes the stairs two at a time.

"Herschel," Rabbi Gold says. "I'm sorry, but I made a mistake. I have given you the wrong reading. You are supposed to read a different passage. I got the weeks mixed up. The reading I gave you is for the next week. But don't worry. In *cheder* tomorrow we will go through the new passage together. You still have nearly a week to learn it."

"Come eat," Mrs. Marks says. Hershy shakes his head. Even the stacks of cakes look revolting.

Several days later Hershy squeezes his eyes shut and mumbles the new words that will transform him into a man. There is just not enough time. Even if he can remember the words, there is *that chant!* Does he go up on this word? How far up? Even the rabbi looks anxious. Hershy prays. He prays for a flood. The river is rising and they are certain to have a flood this spring. Why not now! People will be too busy in a flood to come to a *Bar Mitzvah*. The railroad will be shut down, the roads closed. Everyone will be filling sandbags to make a dike or moving merchandise out of cellars. A flood this week is the answer. Hershy feels God owes him this. After all, if He let the rabbi assign the wrong passage, at the very least He can see that Hershy does not have to suffer the humiliation of being unprepared. Hershy has wondered all his life what magic would change him in one day from a child to a man, and now he is sure that just surviving this ordeal will work the transformation.

"What have you got on your face?" Mrs. Marks asks, pausing in the frosting of an angel cake and running her least-iced finger down Hershy's cheek. "It doesn't come off. You're so red. Have you got a fever?" She clamps her hand on his forehead. "You're burning up!"

Hershy goes to look at himself in the mirror. He feels terrible, but he has felt terrible for days. He is never sick, so he does not believe he can possibly be ill. But, yes, his face is very red, his eyes glazed. His mouth feels dry. He feels sick to his stomach.

"Go to bed," says Mrs. Marks. "I'll bring you some soup."

"No soup," Hershy mumbles. The bed feels wonderful. He falls right asleep and wakes a few hours later to see his mother and old Doc Bosky standing over him. Doc Bosky pops a thermometer into his mouth and holds his wrist.

"Grippe," he announces, after checking Hershy's throat, neck, belly, back, and chest. "La grippe."

"But the *Bar Mitzvah* is tomorrow!" cries Mrs. Marks, as if, under the circumstances, Doc Bosky might revise his diagnosis.

Doc just shrugs. Hershy says to God, "Forget the flood."

It is decided to have everyone come anyway. The food is all prepared after all. Hershy lies in bed and the sounds of high spirits, laughter, plates clattering, glasses clinking, float in the air around him. He can tune in on the conversations of the people who stand near his door or tune out by drifting off to sleep. Morty's father says there is "optimism because of Roosevelt." Mr. Stein agrees that the new President may really do something to overcome the Depression. For an advertising stunt this year Mr. Stein has hired a man to drive blindfolded in a car down Market Street. He was going to rent a freak from the King Brothers Circus, a boy with clock eyes who could rotate his eyes in opposite directions at the same time. However, Mr. Schwartz, the optometrist, got the boy first.

All afternoon friends and relatives peek in and smile or wave or say something consoling. Gifts are piling up—pens, books, handkerchiefs, ties, the accessories of a man. Even a couple of two-and-a-half-dollar gold pieces, and one five-dollar! Plates of dainties are set beside Hershy and he occasionally sips at a glass of punch made of tea and fruit juices. His fever is going down. He feels exhausted, but in a very luxurious way.

He drifts down into one of his brief naps and then is awakened by the sound of a lively discussion in his room. He rolls over and sees Sheldon, Morty, and Nutty trying to work out the arrangement of chessmen in the set that Hershy has just received as a present.

"Maybe we could trade our presents," Morty is saying.

"Hi," Hershy says. His voice sounds like a run-down Victrola.

"Hi," Sheldon says. "How do you feel?"

"Okay."

"Hi, Hersh," Nutty says. "You got six fountain pens."

"That's nothin'," says Sheldon. "My cousin got twelve. Twelve fountain pens."

"Nobody's gonna trade fountain pens either," Morty says. He gets up and comes over to the bed. Crumbs from a flaky *strudel* he is eating float down onto the sheet. Hershy starts to brush them off but lacks the energy.

"Hersh?"

"Yeah?"

"Are you really sick, Hersh?"

"Or what?"

Morty leans down and whispers, "Or are ya fakin'?"

"Ah, yer a nut!" Hershy rolls over and drifts off again.

"So what will happen?" Mrs. Marks asks the rabbi, as the party tapers off.

"So he'll read next week, that's all," says the rabbi.

"Next week!" Hershy nearly jumps out of bed. He hadn't thought about it, but of course he'll have to have a *Bar Mitzvah* anyway. And next week! He knows that passage cold already. It's the one he was assigned by mistake. *Hallelu!* He feels terrific and ready to get out of bed, but Doc Bosky stops in before leaving and says, "Another day in bed should do it. Then a day in the house. By Tuesday you should be a hundred percent. Maybe ninety-nine."

Heads with unseen bodies appear in the doorway and say "Good-bye," "Congratulations," *"Mazel tov."* Dresses rustle by. Many feet go down the stairs. The sounds diminish and resolve into the familiar chatter of dishwashing. Hershy drifts into the comfortable half-sleep of his fever. He wishes there were something he could do for God.

Bar Mitzvah, May 1933

Hershy sneaks a quick look at his new watch as he runs the last lap around the square. He's sure this is the fastest he has ever run the mile. He feels his legs stride out easily. It would only be a small step more to fly. How can he explain how he feels when he runs? His mind is clean, his body magic. Anxieties remain behind. The Valley is unlocked. The square becomes anyplace, anywhere. And the hills—the hills, he notices today—are green, not black. He feels he can, if he wishes, run beyond them.

Temple Israel

Minneapolis, Minnesota

In Honor of the Bar Mitzvah of
JEFFREY MALMON
by His Parents
Mr. & Mrs. Al Malmon

December 30, 1978